The Ventara Adventures:

United We Stand

The Ventara Adventures
United We Stand

Hans David Müller

First Edition

Wet Ink Books
www.WetInkBooks.com
WetInkBooks@gmail.com

The Ventara Adventures: United We Stand
by Hans David Müller

Editor–in–Chief: Richard M. Grove
Editor: Miguel Ángel Olivé Iglesias
Art Director: Richard M. Grove
Chief AI Literary Prompter: Richard M. Grove
Chief AI Art Prompter: Richard M. Grove

Typeset in Calibri
Printed and bound in Canada
Distributed in USA by Ingram,
          – to set up an account – 1-800-937-0152

Library and Archives Canada Cataloguing in Publication

Title: United we stand / Hans David Müller.
Names: Müller, Hans David, author. |
Olivé Iglesias, Miguel Ángel, 1965- editor.
Description: Series statement: The Ventara adventures
Identifiers: Canadiana 2025017474X |
ISBN 9781998324187 (softcover)
Subjects: LCGFT: Science fiction. | LCGFT: Novels.
Classification: LCC PS8626.U44138 U55 2025 |
DDC 813/.6—dc23

Dedicated to
mysupportive wife
Christina
and my
three musketeer kids,
oh and my cat and goat.

Table of Contents

"All for one, and one for all."

This famous phrase is the motto of
the Three Musketeers in the novel
The Three Musketeers
by Alexandre Dumas.
1844 in French
1846 in English

An Introduction
by the Editor,
Miguel Ángel Olivé Iglesias

Dear Readers,

In 2024 I had the opportunity of being the Editor of, *The Ventara Adventures The Resilience of Hope* (Wet Ink Books) by Canadian writer Hans Muller. In my introduction to that novel I said that Muller *"does not let us down."* I resort to that statement once more. *The Ventara Adventures: United We Stand* recaptures the essences of a sci-fi novel with renewed strength adhering to stories and backstories that lure me as a reader and make me jump or shrink or fear or cheer.

Science fiction as a genre is quite diverse. Its themes explore human nature beyond unimaginable frontiers, which expand as far as the vast cosmos. One key side of sci-fi literature is the description of heroes and grand galactic battles of good versus evil. In this new Hans novel, he succeeds in bringing to the spotlight the concept of teamwork—as he highlighted the concept of hope and resilience in his previous one—as well as unity. The very title provides the foundation of what we can expect as readers once we fully immerse in the novel: the phrase—that classic, fervent shout of friendship and mutual support "All for one, and one for all."

Contemporary sci-fi writers aim at offering a picture of struggles on a cosmic level where narratives highlight collaboration and collective endeavors to confront dangers and challenges. Hans Muller follows that line of thought and stresses such idea. Let´s see how he introduces it since the opening paragraph:

> *Captain Kael Ventara, Lieutenant Riz Talon, and Lieutenant Mara Steeler were the embodiment of camaraderie, each a pillar of strength and skill in their own right. Their long-standing friendship, forged by the fires of countless battles, was as strong as the steel of their blades and the hulls of their starship.*

Camaraderie being the clue word (mutual trust and friendly relationship, mutual support, team spirit), we as readers are made aware of an element that will mark the unfolding of the novel. Muller himself knows that even when individual heroes still count, unity and teamwork bring solidity to a cause so the odds of triumph escalate exponentially.

The singular skills of Captain Kael Ventara, Lieutenant Riz Talon, and Lieutenant Mara Steeler, plus the Princess—and the people, contribute to the team's success. It proves how diversity in abilities and a united front can lead to better outcomes. The author places the team in dire situations where their survival depends on sacrificing personal goals for the greater good. This aspect of teamwork is a further step in the notions of heroism that often go to lone individuals defeating the bad guys. This is how Muller describes the characters' spirit of camaraderie and confidence in each other and in collectivism:

> *As the Star Fire sored through open space towards Luna, Kael couldn't shake the feeling that this mission, like so many before, would be far from simple. With his trusted friends by his side, he knew they could handle whatever came their way.*

The consideration of teamwork in sci-fi novels is not totally new. Works such as iconic Isaac Asimov's "Foundation" series presented groups of distinct characters working together to face emergencies. The obvious message was that human power thrives in *association*, as shared intelligence contributes to individual talent.

Muller presents his own version of association towards victory in this quotation:

> *"These three impressive individuals,"*
> *Zane said, his voice strong and clear,*
> *"working as a team, embody the spirit*
> *of 'All for one, and one for all.'*

The motifs of heroes, galactic battles, and teamwork found in science fiction stand as vital reflections on human bonds and group action. Through intense narratives and character development, texts illustrate the power of unity, which is becoming more and more of a defining feature of today's story writing, within and without sci-fi territory. A highly symbolic representation of the feature is noticeable in Muller's depiction of the conference hall:

> *"The seating was arranged in a circular fashion around a central rotating stage, symbolizing the unity and equality of all members."*

Yet, the epitome of the need for unity is much evident in Ambassador Zane's speech:

> *He paused for a moment and let the quiet fill the room. "In the vast expanse of our galaxy, no world stands alone; each is a vital part of the cosmic whole. Together, we embrace the creed of 'All for one, and one for all.' I say, in context with the Galactic Federation 'No nation is an island unto itself.' All members of the Galactic Federation are united in purpose and strength. It is this unity that has allowed us to flourish, to push the boundaries of exploration, and to ensure peace and stability for all."*

Readers will surely relate to his vibrant words, for in them pulsate principles that sign many contemporary societies' aspirations. Where he says that "no world stands alone," we would say that no nation ought to stand alone—because each has resources to share, needs to meet.

Moreover, as social tasks grow progressively difficult, the potential for sci-fi to offer solutions becomes critical. Storylines that focus on teamwork as a prime asset in their plots can educate readers on the importance of shared objectives. Muller sets his panning eye not just on an adult readership; he is looking at youngsters too: motivating them to deal with real-world problems that are oftentimes addressed in isolation by people or nations, might prove promising and may I say *futuristic*, to use a sci-fi term. Societies face excruciating tests, thus the core lessons of collaboration and solidarity in sci-fi literature must continue to echo with optimism and inspire generations to come.

As a reader I was impacted by the clear, warning message sent by Muller through the Ambassador's words again about ominous precedents in history of tyrants and dictators. The author points his finger at Hitler as a reminder of the holocausts and havoc he caused to the human kind:

> *Tiberius is not merely a ruler of his own empire, he is a tyrant that wishes to expand his grip on humanity. He is a power hungry tyrannical dictator in every sense of the word. History has shown us the likes of him before. We need only look to Earth's 20th century, to Adolf Hitler, to understand the destructive path he treads. Hitler, too, rose on a wave of false promises, exploiting the fears and discontent of his people. He manipulated democracy to seize absolute power and then dismantled it piece by piece.*

Notice that Muller contrasts the kind of unity and prosperity he advocates in his novel to that Hitler intended. Including these examples is a fine resource in the author's capacity to link events through history and prompt readers to NOT forget them. But, as we read with contempt about Hitler, Muller also leaves us with a feeling of relief and love when he writes about Gandhi:

There is a strong sense of hopefulness (a major component of Muller's first novel) and faith in tomorrow in the above words. It is valid as a general, worth-minding message and as another effective way to say that the future must always be a bright guiding light or at least we must always fight to make it shine.

Ambassador Zane speaks about unity and shared commitment. Muller guarantees that such ideal is in the characters' public statements as a constant, as a flag that has to be raised high:

> *Quann spoke first, her voice steady but choked with emotion. "This victory is not ours alone. It belongs to every person who resisted. It belongs to every planet and small outpost that dared to join in unity. This victory belongs to everyone who dared to dream of, "All for one, and one for all". Today, we reclaim not just our galaxy, but the ideals that unite us: justice, courage, and hope. Let us rebuild together."*

Princess Quann insists in the role played by *"every person who resisted."* Through her words, the author revisits and reaffirms the goals of *"justice, courage, and hope,"* which have been present in his first novel and in this novel.

The motto "All for one, and one for all" was a vow of unity and camaraderie in Dumas's *The Three Musketeers*. It signified their commitment to stand together in triumph and peril, having loyalty as a top quality. Hans Muller creatively retakes both theme and phrase and regales us his *The Ventara Adventures: United We Stand*. Muller travels momentarily to the 19th century to retrieve for us the motto and all-time themes (friendship and loyalty, honour and chivalry, power and corruption, betrayal and intrigue) and brings all of that to the year 2165.

It is a fresh, enlightening journey of hope, resilience, unity, bravery, optimism, which began with Muller's first novel and he has fruitfully continued here. His closing paragraph is as compelling as his opening one:

> *"And so, the Ventara Adventures came to a close, not as an ending, but as a promise: that unity, courage, and friendship would always prevail. The motto that guided them through every trial remained their beacon: All for one, and one for all."*

As I invited readers in my intro words to Muller's first novel, now I do it again by asking to pilot a spaceship, escort Kael and his friends, go on a new mission this time, put their lives on the line for a victory that will always be welcome, will always be worth going after, for it means peace and prosperity for the people.

Read this second novel with the feeling that whatever dark dangers loom before humanity, love and hope and unity will have to prevail.

Thank you, Hans, once more.

Prof. Miguel Ángel Olivé Iglesias. MSc
Editor

Preface from the Author

Unity, loyalty, and the unwavering pursuit of justice are the bedrock of great endeavors. In the vast expanse of the universe, where civilizations rise and fall, the bonds of camaraderie and shared purpose become the true guiding lights. These ideals, so powerfully articulated in the timeless creed of "All for one, and one for all," transcend time, space, and the limitations of mortal existence. They are a promise, a philosophy, and a rallying cry for those who dare to stand against oppression and forge a path toward a just future.

The essence of unity is not merely the joining of forces but the interweaving of destinies, where individuals find their greatest strength in one another. This sentiment, immortalized in Dumas' classic The Three Musketeers, resonates through generations, reminding us that the fight for justice is not one waged alone. It is fought side by side with those who share our convictions, who bolster our courage in times of doubt, and who remind us that perseverance, even in the darkest of times, is the seed from which hope flourishes.

Philosophically, unity is an act of defiance against the fragmentation of the soul, the dissolution of purpose in the face of adversity. Throughout history, from ancient battlefields to the vast, uncharted frontiers of space, the strength of an alliance has determined the fate of nations and the course of history. The philosopher Hegel viewed the march of history as the unfolding of ideas through struggle and synthesis. In that struggle, it is the united—those bound by trust and principle—who emerge victorious.

The characters within The Ventara Adventures embody this spirit of unity and resilience. Captain Kael Ventara, Lieutenant Riz Talon, and Lieutenant Mara Steeler are more than warriors; they are kindred spirits, each a piece of a greater whole. Through their trials, their victories, and their sacrifices, they prove that true strength is not found in isolation, but in the bonds that tie one to another. Their unwavering loyalty to each other and to the cause of justice forms the very heart of this tale, echoing the philosophy that has guided heroes throughout time.

Their struggle against tyranny is not merely a conflict of firepower and tactics, but a testament to the power of collective hope. In the face of Emperor Dominus Tiberius looming threats, of political machinations and interstellar uncertainty, they stand firm—not because they are invincible, but because they believe in something greater than themselves. Their rallying cry, all for one, and one for all, is not just a battle cry but a declaration of faith in one another, an affirmation that unity can withstand even the most daunting of storms.

At its core, this adventure is a reminder that the universe is not shaped by solitary acts, but by the hands that reach out to lift another up. The Galactic Trio's journey is not just about overcoming enemies, but about proving that, even in the cold vastness of space, no one fights alone. This is a story of perseverance, of brotherhood and sisterhood, of the timeless truth that together, we are greater than the sum of our parts.

And so, as you embark on this journey with Kael, Riz, and Mara, may you find inspiration in their unity, courage in their struggles, and, most importantly, a renewed belief in the boundless power of standing together. For in the face of any challenge, in the vastness of the cosmos or within the trials of our own lives, the creed remains the same: All for one, and one for all.

Happy reading,

Hans David Müller

Trust and camaraderie

are the pillars of true unity.

'All for one, and one for all'

is built on more than friendship.

It is a bond forged through loyalty, sacrifice,

and unwavering support,

ensuring that individuals

stand unbreakable against any storm.

Chapter 1
The Call to Duty

Captain Kael Ventara, Lieutenant Riz Talon, and Lieutenant Mara Steeler were the embodiment of camaraderie, each a pillar of strength and skill in their own right. Their long-standing friendship, forged by the fires of countless battles, was as strong as the steel of their blades and the hulls of their starship.

The three suns of Duneara, the harsh and unrelenting balls of fire, beat down on the planet as they sat in the cool, dimly lit confines of a bar called The Oasis. The irony of the name wasn't lost on them, considering the planet's barren, lifeless deserts. Kael, the native of this arid world, leaned back in his chair, his green eyes twinkling with mischief.

"Alright you bone heads, let's settle this once and for all," Kael laughed out loud, tapping his glass of synthetic whiskey on the stained concrete table. "Are we going to be called the, The Inter-Galactic Trio, The Galactic Trio, or The Three Musketeers?"

Riz, his imposing figure almost comically squeezed into the small chair, scratched his bushy beard. "The Inter-Galactic Trio sounds grand and impressive. We travel between galaxies, after all."

Mara, ever the voice of practicality, rolled her eyes. "It's too long. Galactic Trio is concise and still gets the point across. Plus, we operate mainly in this galaxy."

Kael chuckled. "And the Three Musketeers? It has a certain timeless appeal, doesn't it? 'All for one, and one for all' and all that. Didn't you have to read it when you were in school? It was written by Alexandre Dumas way back in 1844 before they could even fly let alone jump to warp speed. It's a classic name if you ask me."

Riz shook his head. "We're not prancing around with swords and frilly shirts, Kael. We've got plasma rifles and starships. Let's keep our nickname futuristic."

Mara smirked, leaning forward. "How about we take a vote? All in favour of Inter-Galactic Trio?"

Riz enthusiastically raised his hand followed by his second hand waving in the air. His grin widened. Kael and Mara kept their hands down, arms crossed in front.

"The Galactic Trio?" Mara's hand shot up, followed by Kael's after a moment of hesitation.

Riz groaned. "Fine, fine. The Galactic Trio it is. But I reserve the right to grumble about it."

Kael raised his glass. "Agreed. To the Galactic Trio and the trouble we can get up to!"

They clinked glasses, laughter echoing across the small bar.

* * *

Despite the jovial atmosphere, their conversation soon turned to the less appealing aspects of their current location.

"Kael, I still can't believe you chose Duneara for our holiday," Mara said, wiping sweat from her brow. "No beach, no palm trees, no casino, and definitely no nightlife. Just sand, more sand, and oh, did I mention sand?"

Kael shrugged, a sheepish smile on his face. "It's my home planet. I thought you might appreciate a change of scenery."

Riz snorted. "Change of scenery? Kael, if I step outside without protective gear, I get fried. And don't get me started on those mandatory radiation tests every few days."

Mara sighed. "We could've gone to Lumina. Beautiful beaches, perfect weather, and actual nightlife."

Kael spread his hands defensively. "Next time, I promise."

Just then, their comm devices beeped in unison, a shrill tone that cut through their banter. Kael tapped his device, and a holographic image of General Thorne appeared above the table.

"Captain Ventara, Lieutenant Talon, Lieutenant Steeler," Thorne began, his voice as stern and authoritative as ever. "I apologise for interrupting your leave, but we have an urgent mission. Ambassador Zane needs to be escorted to a crucial intergalactic conference on Luna."

The trio exchanged glances. The General's expression left no room for argument.

"Understood, General," Kael replied. "We'll be ready to depart immediately."

Thorne nodded. "Good. Report to the Star Fire and prepare for departure. Thorne out."

The hologram faded, leaving the trio in a momentary silence.

Riz broke the silence with a chuckle. "Thank the lucky stars our glorious holiday has been cut short. Well, this should be an easy-peasy mission. I hope the pay is as good as the other ones."

Mara grinned. "I love babysitting missions, especially when it's Ambassador Zane. He's such a nice guy."

Kael nodded. "Don't forget the mission that was

supposed to be a simple babysitting job taking Ambassador Jones to a meeting on Napol. Even though they are a member of the GF, they have such a suspicious, untrusting nature. Don't you remember we ended up in a firefight with one of their scout ships. We held them off but Star Fire spent three months in a Federation hanger getting fixed up after they shot our caboose off. Ambassador Jones kept yelling, don't fire back, don't fire back, just evade their fire and get out of here. Let's hope this babysitting job is more straight-forward than that."

Mara's eyes widened. "That was a mess. I forget what caused them to be so upset."

Kael leaned back, his expression turning serious. "We were in orbit around Napol, waiting for clearance to land. Suddenly, one of their scout ships accused us of espionage. Before we knew it, they opened fire."

Riz nodded, his face grim. "We had to scramble. Shields up, evasive maneuvers, the whole works. We returned fire, aiming to disable rather than destroy and then Jones started yelling not to fire back. It was a close call."

Mara frowned. "I hate running with our tails between our legs. I would rather fight, and it almost caused Napol to leave the Federation."

Kael sighed. "Yeah, it took months of diplomatic efforts to smooth things over. Let's hope this one goes better."

* * *

The Star Fire, their trusted starship, was a marvel of engineering and design, reflecting the blend of rugged practicality and cutting-edge technology that characterized its crew. As they boarded, Kael couldn't help but feel a rush of pride. This ship had seen them through thick and thin, and now it was time for another adventure.

Riz settled into the pilot's seat, his fingers flying over the controls with practiced ease. "Pre-flight checks complete. All systems go."

Mara took her place at the tactical station, her eyes scanning the readouts. "Weapons and shields are online. We're ready for anything."

Kael, at the command console, tapped the comm. "Star Fire to Galactic Federation Command. We are ready to depart."

General Thorne's voice crackled through the speakers. "Acknowledged, Star Fire. You have clearance for immediate departure. Good luck, and may the stars guide you."

Kael looked at his friends, the camaraderie and trust they shared evident in their eyes. "Let's get Ambassador Zane and show the galaxy what the Galactic Trio can do."

The engines roared to life, and with a smooth lift-off, the Star Fire ascended into the heavens, leaving the harsh sands of Duneara behind.

As they broke through the planet's atmosphere, the view of the stars stretched out before them, a tapestry of infinite possibilities.

"Setting course for Earth," Riz announced with tone of professionalism and excitement.

Kael leaned back, a smile playing on his lips. "Here we go. Another mission, another chance to make a difference."

Mara nodded, her gaze fixed on the stars. "All for one, and one for all."

Kael and Riz echoed the sentiment, their voices buoyant with resilience and unity. "All for one, and one for all."

The Star Fire shot forward, a streak of light against the dark canvas of space, heading towards Earth and the beginning of their next great adventure.

* * *

Arriving on Earth, the Starfire glided into the bustling orbital docking station above the planet. Earth's blue and green expanse shimmered below them, a stark contrast to the harsh landscapes of Duneara.

As they disembarked, they were met by General Thorne in person. "Welcome back, Captain Ventara, Lieutenant Talon, Lieutenant Steeler," he greeted them, his tone formal but warm. "Ambassador Zane is waiting for you in the conference room."

They made their way through the station, passing by windows offering breathtaking views of Earth and the stars beyond. In the conference room, they found Ambassador Zane, a tall, dignified man with silver hair and a well-groomed beard. His piercing blue eyes and the lines etched into his face spoke of wisdom and experience.

"Captain Ventara, Lieutenant Talon, Lieutenant Steeler," Zane greeted them with a nod, his voice calm and measured. "Thank you for taking on this mission."

"It's our honour, Ambassador," Kael replied. "We're ready to ensure your safe passage to Luna."

Zane chuckled with a smile. "As usual I keep hearing good things about you three. When you arrived the landing bay called ahead and said, "The Galactic Trio, have arrived. So you have a moniker now."

Riz grinned. "Yes, that's us. Because we just got dragged off of Duneara I hope this mission is as easy as it sounds."

Zane chuckled. "I certainly hope so, too. But in our line of work, one can never be too sure."

Mara nodded. "We'll be on high alert, Ambassador. Your safety is our top priority."

With that, they escorted Ambassador Zane to the Star Fire. As they prepared for takeoff, Kael addressed his team one last time.

"Alright, team. This might be a babysitting mission, but let's stay sharp. We know how quickly things can go south."

Riz nodded, adjusting the controls. "Roger that, Captain."

Mara took her place at the tactical station, her eyes scanning the readouts. "All systems ready. Let's get this done."

* * *

The Star Fire cruised steadily through the tranquil expanse of space, a journey that spanned several hours as they made their way to Luna. The ship's interior was quiet except for the low hum of the engines and the occasional beep of the navigation systems. With the initial rush of departure behind them, the crew settled into the calm rhythm of the voyage.

Kael stretched in his seat, glancing at Riz and Mara. "We've got time before we arrive. Might as well take it easy for a bit. No point in running ourselves ragged."

Riz leaned back, propping his boots on the console, earning a sharp glance from Mara. "A chance to snooze sounds good. Wake me if we get ambushed by pirates."

Mara chuckled. "You're lucky we haven't installed a shock panel for that console yet."

Across the room, Ambassador Zane sat quietly, his posture relaxed but his eyes thoughtful as he gazed out at the stars. Noticing the lull in conversation, he cleared his throat. "You know, this quiet reminds me of my early days as a Federation Scout."

Kael raised an eyebrow. "You? A scout? I thought you were always in politics."

Zane's laugh was rich and deep. "Hardly. I started just like you, a young, idealistic officer, eager to prove myself. I wasn't much older than you are when I found myself on a barren moon, cut off from my team and facing a squadron of rogue mercenaries."

Riz sat up, suddenly interested. "What happened?"

Zane's eyes gleamed with a mixture of nostalgia and pride. "I was outnumbered, and they had me pinned down in a crater. I had no backup, no communications, and only a standard-issue blaster with a handful of charges left. My first instinct was to fight to the bitter end, but I realised brute force wasn't going to save me."

Mara leaned forward. "What did you do?"

"I studied the terrain, waited for nightfall, and used the shadows to my advantage. I led them on a chase, setting up traps and disabling them one by one. It took all night, but by dawn, I'd taken out their leader and forced the rest to surrender. When my team finally found me, they said it looked like I'd single-handedly fought an army."

Kael whistled low. "That's impressive. You're full of surprises, Ambassador."

Zane shrugged modestly. "Those were different times. Back then, I was as battle-ready as any of you. Life has a way of pushing you down different paths, but the skills you hone and the lessons you learn—those stay with you. Never forget that."

Riz grinned with respect, "You've got more grit than most of the brass I've ever met."

The crew shared a laugh, the camaraderie in the room growing stronger as the Ambassador's story lingered in the air. The journey continued, their bond fortified by shared stories and the knowledge that, regardless of their roles, they were united by a common purpose.

As the Star Fire sored through open space towards Luna, Kael couldn't shake the feeling that this mission, like so many before, would be far from simple. With his trusted friends by his side, he knew they could handle whatever came their way.

The journey to Luna was smooth, the stars gliding past as the Star Fire cruised through the void. As they approached the moon, its silvery surface gleamed against the blackness of space.

"Preparing for landing," Riz announced, his hands deftly maneuvering the controls. "We'll be on Luna in a few minutes."

Kael leaned forward, his gaze fixed on the lunar landscape. "Let's get Ambassador Zane to that conference and make sure everything goes off without a hitch."

Mara nodded, her expression determined. "All for one, and one for all."

As the Star Fire touched down on Luna's surface, the team prepared for the next phase of their mission. Together, they would face whatever challenges awaited them, united in their purpose and strength.

True strength is not found in

individual power alone,

but in the unity of diversity.

Individuality is not weakness;

it is our greatest asset.

When we stand together,

embracing our differences,

we become an unstoppable force,

capable of conquering any challenge.

Chapter 2
Unity in Diversity

The Star Fire landed smoothly on the surface of Luna, Earth's moon, with the bustling cityscape of the orbital docking station around them. The trio disembarked with Ambassador Zane, who was immediately greeted by a swarm of media representatives. Lights flashed and microphones were thrust forward as they approached.

"Ambassador Zane, how do you feel about today's conference?" one media person asked.

Ambassador Zane smiled warmly. "I am here to support the idea of unity among all Galactic Federation members. This conference is a pivotal moment in our shared journey, marking 50 years of collaboration and peace. Our strength lies in our diversity, and I look forward to addressing the assembly to reinforce our commitment to mutual respect and cooperation."

The crowd cheered, and Ambassador Zane continued, "I would like to publicly thank the Galactic Trio for escorting me to this conference." He pointed to Kael, Riz, and Mara, who stood a short distance away, with an expressions of pride that glowed with humility. The crowd turned to look at them, applauding loudly.

"These three impressive individuals," Zane said, his voice strong and clear, "working as a team, embody the spirit of 'All for one, and one for all.' As you will remember they rescued Princess Quann from the tyranny of the self-proclaimed Chancellor Virox and then helped bring Virox not only to his knees but to his end. They have served the Galactic Federation in such a brave and honourable way. They are the perfect exemplification of what the Galactic Federation stands for."

The crowd erupted into cheers again. Zane raised his hand towards Princess Quann, who stood in the crowd. "Thank the stars that she is safe and here today."

Princess Quann, a striking figure with her shoulder-length blonde hair tied back and piercing blue eyes, waved back, her smile radiant. The media captured every moment, broadcasting it live across the galaxy.

As Ambassador Zane walked towards the conference hall, the crowd parted respectfully. Over 400 delegates from every nation in the Galactic Federation filled the large hall. The seating was arranged in a circular fashion around a central rotating stage, symbolizing the unity and equality of all members. The hall was a marvel of architecture, with a dome-shaped ceiling that displayed a holographic representation of the galaxy, reminding everyone of the vastness and diversity of their alliance.

The Master of Ceremonies, a well-known dignitary, stepped onto the stage, his voice amplified to reach every corner of the vast hall. "Thank you all for coming," he began, his voice resonating with warmth and authority. "Today, we gather to celebrate the unity and diversity of the Galactic Federation. For 50 years, we have worked together to promote peace, prosperity, and mutual understanding. This conference is a testament to our collective efforts and our shared commitment to a brighter future."

He paused, allowing the applause to fill the room before continuing. "It is my great honour to introduce someone who needs no introduction. Ambassador Zane has been a pillar of wisdom and leadership within the Galactic Federation. His strategic mind and unwavering dedication to justice and freedom have guided us through many challenges. Please join me in welcoming Ambassador Zane."

The crowd applauded vigorously as Ambassador Zane walked to the centre of the rotating stage. He bowed gently and paused for a moment, looking around the room with a gracious smile, acknowledging the delegates in every direction.

"Ladies and gentlemen, esteemed colleagues, all representatives of the Galactic Federation, and invited intergalactic guests," Zane began, his voice calm and steady, yet crowed with emotion. "Welcome to Luna and her brand new, state-of-the-art orbital docking station. It is the largest of its kind and now orbits as a symbol of what cooperation and unity can accomplish. Today, we stand at a crossroads. For five decades, we have built a federation based on trust, respect, and mutual benefit. Our journey has not been without challenges, but it is through overcoming these obstacles that we have grown stronger."

He paused for a moment and let the quiet fill the room. "In the vast expanse of our galaxy, no world stands alone; each is a vital part of the cosmic whole. Together, we embrace the creed of 'All for one, and one for all.' I say, in context with the Galactic Federation 'No nation is an island unto itself.' All members of the Galactic Federation are united in purpose and strength. It is this unity that has allowed us to flourish, to push the boundaries of exploration, and to ensure peace and stability for all."

"I stand before you today humbled as a proud representative of the Earth Alliance, honoured to address this distinguished assembly on the future of our shared Galactic Federation. As you know, the theme of this conference is 'United We Stand'. This year of 2125 marks a pivotal moment in our journey as a unified interstellar community, now in our 50th year as a united federation. The ongoing growth and evolution of our federation depend on maintaining the collective will that shapes the destiny of countless civilizations.

"Earth's ambitions to continue the colonization of the moons within our Solar System are driven by a vision of prosperity, collaboration, and mutual benefit. As you are already aware, the eight planets in our Solar System are orbited by 222 moons, many of which are rich in natural resources. These resources hold the key to not only our financial stability and security but also the sustained growth and stability of the Galactic Federation as a whole, for centuries to come.

"To date, we have successfully colonized eight of these moons, transforming them into thriving hubs of scientific research, commerce, and culture. However, this is merely the beginning. Our plans for the next decade include the colonization of eight additional moons, each chosen for its unique potential to contribute to our collective advancement.

"These moons harbor abundant natural resources, including water, minerals, and rare elements essential for technological innovation and development. By tapping into these resources, we can ensure the economic vitality and energy independence of the Galactic Federation. Moreover, the scientific knowledge gained from these endeavours will propel us toward new frontiers of understanding and discovery.

"Let me be clear: our intentions are not driven by greed or a desire for domination. We are peacemakers, not agitators of nations. We are builders of harmony, not conquerors of worlds. We are negotiators of agreements, not dictators of policies. We are supporters of assets, not pickpockets or burglars of sovereign resources.

"Our commitment to peaceful exploration and mutual respect remains unwavering. The Earth Alliance seeks to foster collaboration and unity among all member states of the Galactic Federation. We believe that by working together, we can overcome the challenges that lie ahead and create a future where every civilization thrives.

"The colonization of these moons is not merely an Earth Alliance initiative; it is the undeniable evidence of the spirit of cooperation that defines the Galactic Federation of which we are all members. We invite all member states to join us in this noble endeavour, to share in the benefits of these resources, and to contribute to the collective well-being of our galaxy.

"In closing, let us reaffirm our dedication to the principles of peace, harmony, and collaboration. Let us seize this opportunity to build a brighter future for all. Together, we can ensure that the light of integrity and loyalty continues to shine, even in the darkest of times. In the spirit of 'All for One, and One for All,' I finish the quote, 'united we stand divided we fall.' coined by the Earth literary genius Alexandre Dumas in 1844, and echoing the wisdom of John Donne, who wrote in 1624 in his famous Meditation XVII, 'No man is an island, entire of itself; every man is a piece of the continent, a part of the main.' Both of these profound men highlighted the interconnectedness of humanity and the importance of solidarity. We will continue to overcome all forms of tyranny and every attempt to overturn our progress as a united federation.

"In the spirit of those two great visionary men of centuries past, I stand before you as an Ambassador of the Earth Alliance and pledge our commitment to the divine Principle as the foundation of the Galactic Federation: In the vast expanse of our intergalactic space, no world stands alone; each is a vital part of the cosmic whole. Together, we embrace the creed of 'United We Stand', and no nation is an island unto itself. All members of the Galactic Federation are united in purpose and strength."

Ambassador Zane's words resonated deeply with the audience, their smiles and nods of approval showing their agreement. "Our mission does not end here. We must continue to support one another, to stand together against any threat to our collective peace. We must foster innovation, encourage dialogue, and uphold the values that have brought us this far."

The delegates cheered and stomped their feet in unison, a sign of union and solidarity. Zane bowed in every direction, his eyes meeting those of the delegates, each bow a gesture of respect and gratitude.

"Thank you," he concluded, his voice rich with genuine warmth. "Together, we will continue to build a future where every civilization thrives. All for one, and one for all."

The applause was thunderous as Zane left the stage, his heart overflowed with hope and resolve. He knew that with such unity, the Galactic Federation could overcome any challenge that lay ahead.

As he exited the stage, the Galactic Trio were there to greet him. They guided him through the throngs of well-wishers and admirers, ushering him to a private anteroom. The room was quiet, a stark contrast to the lively conference hall, offering a moment of respite.

"That was a magnificent speech, Ambassador," Kael said with great admiration.

Riz nodded, grinning. "You had them hanging on every word."

Mara added, "And you gave us quite the shout-out. We appreciate it."

Alone, our efforts are but whispers

in the wind, small and fleeting.

But when we unite with allies,

our voices become a chorus,

our strength multiplies,

and no obstacle is insurmountable.

Together,

we achieve what once seemed impossible.

Chapter 3
The Princess's Plight

Princess Quann sat in her hotel room on Luna, reflecting on the events of the day. The conference had been inspiring, with Ambassador Zane delivering a powerful speech that resonated with every delegate. She felt a sense of optimism about the future of the Galactic Federation, yet there was an underlying tension she couldn't shake off.

A soft sound broke her thoughts. She glanced at the door and noticed a small note that had been slipped under it. Picking it up, she unfolded the paper and read the hurriedly scrawled message:

"I admire you and what you are doing on your home world of Lumina, so I have to inform you that I overheard someone at the conference talking about a plot to discredit you and overthrow the Lumina sector. It was Emperor Dominus Tiberius, but I don't know the other person.

He was short and weak-looking with long grey hair. He had a delegation badge, but I could not see the name."

Quann's heart raced as she clutched the note tightly, her thoughts swirling. The words on the paper confirmed her worst fears—the looming threat was not just a vague notion but a real and imminent danger. The mention of Emperor Dominus Tiberius sent a chill down her spine. His reputation for ruthless tactics was known across the galaxy, and if he was involved in a plot to discredit her and destabilize the Lumina sector, the consequences could be catastrophic.

She paced the room, her mind racing through possible courses of action. Panic threatened to cloud her judgment, but Quann forced herself to focus. She was not just a princess but a leader, and her people depended on her to navigate this crisis. The cryptic details about the short, weak-looking man with long grey hair and a delegation badge gnawed at her. Who was he? Why would he align with Dominus Tiberius? The mystery only deepened her sense of urgency.

Quann knew she couldn't handle this alone. She needed guidance, someone she could trust implicitly, someone with the wisdom to see through the shadows of deceit. One name came to her mind immediately: Ambassador Zane. Known for his strategic brilliance and unwavering loyalty to the principles of justice, Zane had been a steadfast ally of Lumina for years. If anyone could help her unravel this conspiracy and determine the best course of action, it was him.

Without hesitation, Quann decided to seek his counsel. She scribbled a quick note and handed it to her trusted aide, instructing him to arrange a private meeting with the ambassador at the earliest opportunity. As the night wore on, she sat by the window, her gaze fixed on the stars. Lumina's light had always been a beacon of hope, and she vowed to protect it at any cost.

The next morning, Princess Quann arrived at the conference hall before dawn, the weight of responsibility heavy on her shoulders. She moved with purpose, her expression firm. When she reached Ambassador Zane's office, she knocked softly but firmly.

"Come in," a deep, reassuring voice called out.

Quann entered to find the Ambassador seated at his desk, his presence exuding calm authority. He rose and greeted her with a warm smile, his sharp eyes studying her intently. "Princess Quann, it's always a pleasure to see you, though I know this isn't a social call. I got the note that your aid delivered last night."

"You're right, Ambassador," she said, her voice steady but edged with urgency. "As you know from my note, I've come because a grave threat has emerged, and I need your advice."

Zane gestured for her to sit, his expression growing serious. "Tell me everything," he said. "Together, we will find a way to protect Lumina and expose the truth."

* * *

Kael, Riz, and Mara were promptly called to Ambassador Zane's office. They entered with their usual confident demeanor, but the sight of Princess Quann's worried face made them immediately serious.

"Princess Quann," Kael began, his tone respectful. "How can we assist you?"

Quann explained the situation, showing them the note. "I need your help to uncover this conspiracy and protect the Lumina sector."

Riz's eyes narrowed. "A plot against you and Lumina? By Tiberius? This won't stand."

Mara placed a hand on Quann's arm. "We're with you, Princess. All for one, and one for all."

Kael nodded. "We need a plan. First, we should identify the unknown accomplice. A short, weak-looking man with long grey hair and a delegation badge shouldn't be too hard to spot."

Zane added, "We also need to ensure that our investigation doesn't disrupt the conference or undermine the delegates' confidence in the Federation."

The group huddled together, discussing their strategy. They decided to split up and discreetly gather information. Kael and Mara would mingle with the delegates, listening for any suspicious conversations, while Riz would use his technical skills to monitor communications and access restricted areas if necessary.

* * *

The conference hall buzzed with activity as delegates from across the galaxy gathered for the second day of discussions. The Galactic Trio moved through the crowd, their eyes and ears alert for any clues.

Kael struck up a conversation with a group of delegates from various sectors, subtly steering the topic toward recent events and political intrigues. Mara, meanwhile, engaged in casual chats, her sharp eyes scanning the crowd for the described accomplice.

Riz, stationed at a security terminal, skillfully accessed the communication logs and surveillance feeds. He noted any unusual activity and reported back to the team.

Hours passed with no significant leads until Mara spotted a man fitting the description in a quiet corner, speaking to a delegate from Napol. She subtly signaled to Kael, who made his way over, blending into the crowd.

* * *

As Kael approached, he overheard snippets of their conversation. The man with long grey hair was expressing concern about the Federation's influence on the Lumina sector. Kael moved closer, catching more details.

"...the plan must proceed. Emperor Tiberius cannot afford to fail this time," the man said.

Kael noted the man's badge: President Larkus Loanus of the Zetarian Empire, an ally of Tiberius. He quietly relayed the information to Mara and Riz from his com badge.

* * *

Back in Zane's office, the team reconvened to share their findings.

"President Loanus is the accomplice," Kael confirmed. "He's conspiring with Tiberius to undermine Princess Quann."

Zane nodded, his expression grave. "We must expose Loanus, but we need evidence. Riz, can you retrieve the surveillance footage of their conversation?"

Riz grinned. "Already on it, Ambassador." He pulled up the footage on his device, capturing the crucial moments.

Quann sighed in relief. "With this evidence, we can confront Loanus privately and thwart their plans without causing a scene."

* * *

The Galactic Trio approached President Loanus after he stepped away from a conversation with a fellow delegate. Captain Ventara put his hand on President Loanus' shoulder and guided him a few step away to a secluded area, away from the main conference activities. In a soft but firm voice Captain Ventara leaned forward, "President Loanus, Ambassador Zane requested that we escort you to a private meeting room just down the hall. Please follow Lieutenant Steeler. She will lead the way." The four of them walked calmly to meet Ambassador Zane.

Ambassador stood with his arms crossed, his presence commanded respect, and Loanus looked visibly nervous. "President Loanus," Ambassador Zane began, his tone firm. "You are a valued member of the GF. I personally voted to include The Zetarian Empire in the Federation when you applied six years ago. I understand that soon after you joined, the Federation supported your mining operation with a four billion dollar contract to purchase ore to help get the operation up and running. Before the conference I investigated how your new water reclamation plant is working out for you. I think the Federation funded 60% of the building costs and we are in negotiation with you to possibly forgive half of that loan. How are things going in The Zetarian Empire over all? Are you having any problems or complications that we should know about?"

President Larkus Loanus stood awkwardly running his hand through his long grey hair, "What is this about, Ambassador Zane? You have never given me the time of day in the past and now you bring me into a private meeting escorted by these three thugs. It feels like something is up."

Ambassador Zane stepped a bit closer to President Larkus Loanus and, put his hands on his hips, "Nothing's up, nothing's wrong, we at the Federation just want to make sure that everything is ok for you and The Zetarian Empire. It is just that we are aware of your covert plot with Emperor Tiberius against Princess Quann and the Lumina sector. We have evidence of your conversations."

President Loanus paled. "I-I don't know what you're talking about."

Ambassador Zane smiled and stepped even closer, "You see we at the Federation are not as stupid as you and Emperor Dominus Tiberius think we are. Captain, show our dear friend what you have.

Kael stepped forward, showing the surveillance footage on his device. "Denying it won't help. We have proof and this is not the only proof that we have."

Ambassador Zane smiled at President Loanus again, "Let me speak plainly, you have two choices: cooperate and explain your actions, or face the embarrassing and financial consequences of financial ruin for your country when we not only pull all of our financial support but crush your infrastructure in the process and you being removed from office by your people, you can hope you are not lynched."

President Loanus glanced around, realizing he had no escape. He sighed in defeat. "Fine. I'll talk."

* * *

President Loanus sat hard into a chair and confessed his involvement with Tiberius. "Emperor Tiberius threatened me and my family and promised me resources and power if I helped him discredit Princess Quann and destabilize Lumina. I never thought it would go this far."

Zane's expression softened slightly. "You must renounce your alliance with Tiberius and publicly support Princess Quann and Lumina. This is the only way to make amends and avoid further repercussions."

President Loanus nodded, clearly shaken. "I will. I'll do whatever it takes to rectify this but don't blame me for the bigger picture. You have no idea what Emperor Tiberius is capable of or what he has up his sleve. You think that pulling me down with the tug of the Federation chain is going to solve your problems. Emperor Tiberius has been planning something much bigger for years and before you ask or try to put the bite on me, I don't know anything. All I know is that I was just the tiny cog in the wheel of Emperor

Dominus Tiberius thinking he can be the Emperor of the entire Federation so keep your eyes open, you bunch of idiots."

* * *

The next day, President Loanus publicly declared his support for Princess Quann and Lumina, denouncing his previous alliance with Tiberius. The delegates, initially surprised, quickly rallied behind Princess Quann, strengthening her position and ensuring the stability of the Lumina sector.

Ambassador Zane and the Galactic Trio watched from the sidelines, satisfied with the outcome.

"We did it," Mara said, a smile breaking through her serious demeanor.

Kael nodded. "All for one, and one for all."

Riz chuckled. "And one less threat to worry about."

Princess Quann approached them, her expression one of deep gratitude. "Thank you. Your bravery and quick thinking saved my sector and my reputation."

Zane placed a hand on her shoulder. "It was a team effort, Princess. Together, we stand strong."

The Galactic Trio and Princess Quann shared a moment of solidarity, their bond strengthened by the challenges they had overcome. As they looked out at the assembled delegates, they knew that their work was far from over, but with unity and sheer willpower, they could face any challenge the galaxy threw their way.

In the face of dissent,

unity becomes our strongest shield.

Every challenge of rebellion can be met with

harmony,

for true strength lies not in division,

but in standing together,

turning discord into resilience

and chaos

into lasting peace.

Chapter 4
Ambush at the Conference

The grand hall of the Intergalactic Council was a sight to behold. The culmination of two days of intense deliberations, heated debates, and heartfelt speeches had left the room vibrated with a palpable sense of harmony and joy. As the final speech concluded, delegates from star systems far and wide, once strangers or even rivals, embraced each other in spontaneous handshakes and hugs. The camaraderie in this hall was a testament to the harmony within the Galactic Federation; the federation was indeed in good shape.

The conference had been a resounding success, and the transformation of the hall into a banquet venue happened swiftly. Tables laden with a variety of foods and drinks from every nation replaced the conference tables. As earth's culinary contribution, at the centre of the hall, stood a magnificent chocolate fondue, lavishly cascading a river of chocolate surrounded by decadent bowls of fruit. Nearby, a pyramid of wine glasses shimmered atop an under-lit glass table, casting dazzling reflections across the room. A laser light display danced on every wall, adding to the festive atmosphere. Partners, spouses, and guests of the delegates began to arrive, their laughter and chatter blending into the joyous symphony of the celebration.

The Galactic Trio stood at different spots in the room, triangulated so they could each see the others at a glance. They mingled with the crowd, attempting to blend in as guests, but their true role was to maintain security and respond to any potential threats. The stakes were high, and they knew they had to remain vigilant.

Kael, standing near the chocolate fondue, watched as a delegate from the Orion Cluster dipped a strawberry into the flowing chocolate, laughing as his wife playfully teased him about the mess he made. Kael smiled, but his eyes scanned the room, ever watchful.

Riz, positioned near the entrance, exchanged pleasantries with a group of delegates from the Andromeda Sector. He kept one hand casually resting on the hilt of his blaster, hidden beneath his cloak. His sharp eyes took in every detail, every movement, ready to spring into action.

Mara, near the wine glasses pyramid, chatted with Princess Quann, who had just arrived. Quann's presence drew many admiring glances and heartfelt congratulations from the delegates. Mara's plasma shield generator was hidden in plain sight as a decorative bracelet on her wrist, ready to activate at a moment's notice.

The celebration was in full swing when suddenly, a commotion erupted near the entrance. The room fell silent as a group of heavily armed mercenaries burst into the hall, their blasters trained on Ambassador Zane and Princess Quann. The leader of the mercenaries, a fearsome figure with a scar running down his face, barked orders, demanding the surrender of Ambassador Zane and Princess Quann. All five of the well-armed terrorists shot echoing blasts into the ceiling. Shouts and shrieks of fear echoed through the room. The leader of the group yelled in a menacing voice, "Give us Ambassador Zane and Princess Quann immediately or everyone dies."

"Everyone, get down!" Kael shouted, his voice cutting through the stunned silence. In an instant, he sprang into action, his energy blade igniting with a hiss as it sliced through the air. He moved with the precision and grace of a seasoned warrior, engaging the mercenary leader in a fierce duel.

Riz, with his dual blasters drawn, provided cover fire. He moved with deadly efficiency, taking down attackers with pinpoint accuracy. His blasters fired in rapid succession, each shot finding its mark.

Mara, activating her plasma shield, deftly deflected incoming shots. She moved protectively toward Princess Quann, shielding her from the attackers. "Stay close, Your Highness," she instructed, her voice calm and steady.

The trio moved with practiced coordination, a seamless blend of agility and strength. Kael's energy blade clashed with the mercenary leader's weapon, sparks flying with each strike. The leader was skilled, but Kael's grit and training gave him the upper hand.

Riz's blasters blazed, taking down mercenaries who tried to flank them. "Watch your left, Mara!" he called out, his voice clear and precise.

Mara's shield absorbed the brunt of the assault, her movements fluid as she protected the delegates. She spotted a shadowy figure slipping into the room, attempting to use the distraction to strike at Ambassador Zane and Princess Quann. "Kael, to your right!" she alerted.

Kael, with his keen senses, intercepted the would-be assassin. He disarmed the attacker with a swift maneuver, his energy blade slicing through the air with deadly precision. "Not today," he muttered, his eyes cold and determined. The skirmish lasted for less than fifteen minutes. Most of the members of the party had escaped from the room or were hiding under tables.

The trio's efforts were relentless. One by one, the mercenaries fell, their attack thwarted by the trio's exceptional combat skills. It was a miracle that no one was hurt other than the four dead assailants. As the dust settled, Kael approached the captured mercenary leader lying face down, arms secured at his back. Kael's blade was still active and glowing. Yanking him to his feet, he growled, "Who sent you?" His voice was low and menacing, a dangerous edge cutting through the silence of the hall.

The leader defiantly resisted, struggling against Kael's firm grip around his neck. "You don't think we are going to find out who directed you?" Kael hissed, tightening his hold. The mercenary's eyes blazed with defiance, but the pain in his expression was unmistakable. Kael's grip didn't falter, his eyes boring into the mercenary's soul. "Talk!" Kael demanded, shaking him roughly. The room was tense, every delegate holding their breath, watching the interrogation unfold.

The mercenary gasped for breath, his resistance wavering. "You're wasting your time," he spat, but the quiver in his voice betrayed his fear. Kael didn't relent, his grip like iron, his presence intimidating. The captured assailant's defiance began to crumble under the unyielding pressure. "Who sent you?" Kael repeated, his voice a dangerous whisper. "Your four comrades are dead, including your captain. I recognise him from wanted bulletins. We have already secured your ship at docking bay twenty-two, and we have your communication database. It is only a matter of a few minutes before we know everything." Kael's threat to throw him out of the airlock shuddered through the mercenary. "We know that you are just a private taking orders, so save your skin now before the officials get their hands on you."

Finally, the captive broke, his strength of mind shattered by Kael's intense gaze and unrelenting grip. "Okay, okay, you are right, I was just following orders. We all were. No one has any personal alliance with Emperor Tiberius. We are just conscripted military. We were all drafted against our will." the mercenary confessed, his voice a defeated whisper. "He wanted Ambassador Zane and Princess Quann captured alive as leverage to disrupt more than the conference. He wanted to eliminate any hope of the alliance expanding. You have to take me into protective custody. Emperor Tiberius has men stationed all through your precious Federation. They will kill me if you don't put me in protective custody."

The revelation sent shockwaves through the hall. Delegates murmured in disbelief and outrage, realizing the depth of the conspiracy. Princess Quann, with her characteristic grace, stepped forward to address the assembly.

"Today, we have witnessed the lengths to which our enemies will go to sow discord and chaos," she declared, her voice resonating with strength. "But we will not be intimidated. We will stand united against tyranny and fight for our freedom."

Ambassador Zane, visibly shaken but unyielding, nodded in agreement. "The evidence is clear. Emperor

Dominus Tiberius seeks to undermine our efforts for peace. We must be vigilant and unwavering in our resolve."

The Galactic Trio stood by, their mission accomplished but knowing that the road ahead would be fraught with danger. The ambush had been thwarted, but the battle against the Emperor's treachery was far from over. With renewed resolve, they vowed to continue their fight for justice and liberty, no matter the cost.

The celebration, now tinged with a newfound resolve, continued. Delegates, though shaken, found solace in their unity and the strength of their collective resolve. The Galactic Trio, ever watchful, knew that their journey was far from over. They had uncovered a critical piece of the puzzle, but the conspiracy ran deep. Their fight for freedom and justice would continue, driven by the hope and courage they saw in the eyes of those they had sworn to protect.

When we stand united with new allies,

our strength transcends boundaries,

our resolve becomes unshakable,

and no force in the galaxy

can break the will of unity.

Together,

we are a force

of unwavering determination,

unstoppable in the face of any challenge.

Chapter 5

Mercenaries Escape to the Stars

The echoes of the final skirmish still reverberated through the conference hall as the Galactic Trio—Kael Ventara, Riz Talon, and Mara Steeler—gathered their thoughts. The mercenaries, though defeated, had revealed a disturbing truth: more enemies lurked in the shadows.

"As it turns out, there were more mercenaries hidden in the corridors leading to the conference room," Kael said, his voice grim. "They were positioned as a support team to fight their way off Luna after capturing Ambassador Zane and Princess Quann."

Mara nodded, her sharp gaze scanning the room for any remaining threats. "And they have two more starships in orbit. We didn't capture those after the conference room skirmish like we did with the docked ship."

Riz, ever the tactician, stepped forward. "Then we need to move fast. Those mercenaries in the corridors will try to escape to their ships. If they get away, we'll have a bigger problem on our hands."

Without hesitation, the trio rushed into the winding corridors of the conference facility, their footsteps echoing in the vast, empty space. The mercenaries, realizing their cover was blown, fled toward the docking bay, but the Galactic Trio was hot on their heels.

* * *

The corridors were a maze of steel and glass, the dim emergency lights flickering sporadically. The Galactic Trio's pursuit was relentless. Kael led the way, his energy blade humming with an eerie blue glow. Riz and Mara followed, their blasters at the ready.

"There they are!" Mara shouted, pointing to a group sprinting toward the docking bay.

Kael increased his pace, his blade slicing through the air as he charged forward. Riz and Mara provided cover, their blasters firing precise shots to keep the combatants at bay.

The mercenaries, realizing they were outmatched, scattered in different directions, but the Galactic Trio moved with precision. Kael engaged the closest soldier as he charged at him, their weapons clashing into a shower of sparks. Riz and Mara took down the others with ruthless efficiency.

"We can't let them reach their ships!" Riz barked, his voice reverberating through the corridor.

Kael nodded, his eyes fixed on their targets. "Mara, take the left flank. Riz, cover the right. I'll handle the front."

The trio split, each moving with the precision of a well-oiled machine. Mara's agility let her outmaneuver the mercenaries on the left, her blaster shots finding their marks with deadly accuracy. Riz's imposing presence ensured no mercenary could break past his position. Kael's energy blade moved like lightning, cutting through enemy defences with lethal grace.

Despite their efforts, a group of five managed to reach the docking bay and board their starships. The engines roared to life, and the ships began to lift off.

"Riz, get us to the Star Fire! We're not letting them escape," Kael ordered, his voice sharp with urgency.

Riz didn't hesitate. The trio bolted toward the hangar, sprinting up the boarding ramp of the Star Fire as the ship's systems powered up. Kael slammed into the captain's seat, his eyes locked on the fleeing enemy ships.

The Star Fire's engines ignited, shaking the docking bay as it rocketed into the darkness.

"The chase is on," Kael muttered.

Loyalty is the anchor

that holds alliances firm,

even in the fiercest tempests.
True unity is not merely standing side by side

in triumph but holding fast

in trials and adversity.

When trust binds us,

no betrayal can shatter our strength,
and no enemy can break our will.

Chapter 6
The Hidden Fortress

Kael gripped the console as the Star Fire surged after the escaping star ships. Their opportunity to stop them was closing fast.

"Mara, scan for their flight path," he ordered.

She didn't need to be told twice. If those ships reached their reinforcements, this chase would turn into a battle they couldn't win.

Riz, the best pilot in the galaxy, took the controls, his hands moving with effortless precision. Mara manned the tactical station, her fingers flying across the interface. Kael stood at the command console, his mind focused on the hunt.

"They're fast, but we're faster," Riz muttered, adjusting the thrusters.

Mara's eyes flicked to the tactical screen. "Incoming transmission from the enemy ships. They're calling for reinforcements."

Kael's jaw tightened. "We need to intercept them before their backup arrives. Riz, push the engines to max. Mara, power up the weapons."

The Star Fire streaked through the void, its sleek frame cutting through the darkness. The two mercenary ships burned bright ahead, their engines glowing like fiery comets.

"Locking onto targets," Mara reported. "Ready to fire on your command, Captain."

Kael's fingers curled into a fist. "Fire at will."

The Star Fire's cannons blazed, streaks of energy lancing toward the enemy ships. The first mercenary vessel shuddered under the impact, its shields flickering and failing. The second ship veered sharply, trying to evade, but Riz's piloting skills were unmatched.

"We've got them," Riz said with a grin as Mara unleashed another barrage.

But just as victory seemed within reach, the alarms blared.

"Two more enemy ships inbound," Mara warned. "Reinforcements."

Kael clenched his fists. They were outnumbered.

"We need to find refuge," he said. "There's an old Galactic Federation refueling station nearby. It's rarely used, but it might be our only chance."

Riz nodded, adjusting the course. "Hang on. This is going to be a rough ride."

* * *

The Star Fire streaked through space, its engines burning at full throttle. The refueling station loomed ahead—a relic from a bygone era, floating alone in the abyss.

As they approached, Riz sent a hail. "This is the Star Fire requesting emergency docking clearance."

A moment later, a voice crackled through the speakers. "Star Fire, this is Hank. You're clear to dock. What's the emergency?"

"We're being pursued by enemy ships," Riz replied. "We need a place to hide."

"Understood," Hank's voice was calm and reassuring. "Hurry up and get in here."

The Star Fire swooped into the docking bay, its engines powering down as the bay doors sealed shut behind them. Outside, the enemy ships circled like hungry predators.

* * *

Inside, the Galactic Trio met Hank, a grizzled station manager with a weathered face and sharp eyes.

"Welcome to my humble outpost," Hank said with a chuckle. "I've seen a lot, but not many like you."

Kael shook his hand. "Thanks for the help, Hank. We needed a place to lay low."

Hank smirked. "You got it. This station may be old, but it's got a few tricks left. You're safe for now."

Mara eyed the aging control panels. "We appreciate it. But those ships won't wait out there forever."

Riz nodded. "We need a plan. We can't stay here indefinitely."

Kael's mind was already working. "First, let's make sure this station is secure. Then, we'll figure out our next move."

* * *

The control room was a mix of old and new tech, dusty monitors flickering as they displayed the enemy ships. Hank leaned back in his chair, studying them.

"These old eyes have seen a lot," he mused. "But I've never seen a crew as determined as you three."

Kael studied the monitors. "They won't wait forever. We need to deal with them."

Riz tapped the console. "We could try to outmaneuver them, but they outnumber us."

Mara's eyes narrowed. "We need to use our surroundings. This station might have hidden defences."

Hank's lips curled into a grin. "You know, you might be onto something. This place was built for war. We've got surprises for unwelcome guests."

Kael smirked. "Show us."

Hank led them through the station, revealing hidden turrets and reinforced bulkheads. The Galactic Trio quickly formulated a strategy, integrating the station's defences.

* * *

As the enemy ships circled, Kael, Riz, and Mara prepared for the inevitable attack.

"Let's give them a welcome they won't forget," Kael said.

The enemy ships opened fire—but the hidden turrets sprang to life, returning fire with deadly accuracy.

Riz maneuvered the Star Fire alongside, using its cannons to support the defence. Mara targeted weak points, her tactical brilliance turning the tide.

The battle raged, but the station's firepower proved overwhelming. One by one, the enemy ships were disabled or destroyed, their wreckage drifting into the void like shattered remains of a failed ambush. The last surviving vessel, its hull scorched and engines flickering, turned tail and fled into the abyss, vanishing in a blur of light.

A tense silence filled the control room before Hank threw his hands up, laughing. "This old station still has what it takes! That's enough wreckage to keep me salvage-picking for two years. I'll make a bundle selling the scrap."

Mara exhaled, lowering her blaster as she watched the drifting debris. "They won't be bothering us again anytime soon."

Riz smirked, leaning back in his seat. "Next time, they should think twice before messing with a so-called 'abandoned' station."

Kael grinned, stepping away from the console. "Glad we could help." He clapped Hank on the shoulder. "And I have a feeling you just became a very rich man."

Hank chuckled, rubbing his hands together. "Oh, you bet. Now, let's crack open a drink and talk about what you fine folks are planning next."

All for one, and one for all,

is more than a creed,

it is a vow of unity and commitment.

It calls us to stand together, fight as one,

and lift each other up

in every challenge we face

no matter how big or small.

Chapter 7
The Return to Luna

The engines of the Star Fire roared to life as the Galactic Trio embarked on their journey back to Luna. The stars stretched out before them, a shimmering tapestry of possibilities. The starship battle at the old refueling station with the help of Hank ended as a resounding success but they needed to regroup with Ambassador Zane and Princess Quann to strategize their next move.

As they approached Luna, the sight of the moon's silvery surface brought a sense of calm. The orb was a beacon of hope in the vast expanse of space. Yet, as they neared their destination, Kael received a transmission from General Thorne, the stern but respected leader of the Galactic Federation Forces.

"Captain Ventara," General Thorne's voice crackled through the comm system, "We've established a temporary headquarters on the military base orbiting Luna. We'll debrief there. Report as soon as possible."

"Understood, General," Kael replied, his tone steady. "We're a few light hours away. Expect us shortly."

* * *

The military base orbiting Luna buzzed with activity. Starships of various sizes docked in precision, while soldiers moved in unison, their purpose clear in every stride. Though temporary and somewhat antiquated, the base was equipped with advanced technology, standing as evidence to the Federation's adaptability under pressure. It was here that the seeds of rebellion against Emperor Dominus Tiberius would take root.

As the Star Fire landed in the designated bay, Kael, Riz, and Mara disembarked to find General Thorne waiting for them. The General was a towering figure, his presence commanding respect. His short-cropped salt-and-pepper hair and the scars on his face spoke of a lifetime of service and battles fought.

"Welcome back," General Thorne greeted them, his green eyes sharp and assessing. "Ambassador Zane and Princess Quann are already inside. Follow me."

The bustling corridors were alive with anticipation, a blend of organised chaos and hope. Soldiers saluted as the trio passed. Despite a heavy sense of weariness they projected a sense of drive and fortitude as they saluted back. In the command room, Ambassador Zane and Princess Quann were engaged in a discussion. Zane, with his dignified silver hair and piercing blue eyes, exuded an air of wisdom and authority. Princess Quann, her blonde hair tied back and her blue eyes glowing with the power of conviction, stood tall, embodying strength and resilience.

"Captain Ventara, Lieutenant Talon, Lieutenant Steeler," Zane greeted them each with a warm handshake. "Thank you for your swift actions. We've much to discuss."

Kael nodded. "It's good to see you both safe. What's the current situation?"

General Thorne gestured to a holographic map of the galaxy. "We've received intelligence that Emperor Dominus Tiberius is mobilizing his forces in the Napol sector. We need to formulate a strategy to counter this threat."

Princess Quann stepped forward, her expression grave. "The Lumina sector is particularly vulnerable," she began, her voice steady but laced with concern. "Tiberius has long coveted its resources and strategic position, and for good reason. One of our moons, Auralis, is unique in the galaxy—rich with deposits of garium ore, a substance so rare and potent that it has become the cornerstone of advanced technology and energy systems throughout the interstellar realms.

"Garium isn't just a resource; it's the lifeblood of innovation. It powers our starships, fuels our planetary defence systems, and is even critical for medical advancements that save countless lives. Its energy output is unparalleled, and a single ton of refined garium can sustain an entire planetary grid for decades. If Tiberius were to seize control of Auralis, he would gain not only immense wealth but also an unassailable advantage in energy production and military capability.

"For Lumina, this garium isn't just an asset—it's our future. It ensures our independence, strengthens our alliances, and supports the livelihood of millions who depend on the trade and development it fuels. But to Tiberius, it's a weapon, a means to tighten his grip on the galaxy and crush any resistance to his rule. We must protect Auralis at all costs, for if its garium falls into the wrong hands, the balance of power could shift irreversibly, plunging the galaxy into darkness."

"I didn't know that garium was such a core of your wealth", Mara glanced at the map, her mind racing. "We have to protect Auralis at all cost. What about our allies? Can we count on their support?"

Ambassador Zane nodded. "We've reached out to the Galactic Federation members. Many have pledged their support, but we must be prepared for those who might waver under Tiberius's influence."

Riz crossed his arms, his gaze intense. "What's our first move, General?"

Thorne's voice was firm. "We need to reinforce our defences around Lumina and gather intelligence on Tiberius's plans. I've already dispatched reconnaissance teams, but we need more eyes on the ground."

Kael turned to Quann. "Princess, you know the Lumina sector better than anyone. Any insights you can share will be invaluable."

Quann nodded, her expression determined. "The Lumina sector is rich in natural resources, which Tiberius aims to exploit. We have strong defences, but we must bolster them. Additionally, political rivalries within the sector could be a weakness if Tiberius seeks to exploit them."

Zane interjected. "We also need to ensure that the Lumina sector's leadership remains united. Divided, we fall."

* * *

The hours that followed were a blur of strategic planning. The command room buzzed with activity as transmissions were sent, reports analysed, and plans refined. Kael, Riz, and Mara immersed themselves in their respective roles. Kael worked closely with Thorne to coordinate troop movements and supply lines. Riz monitored communications, intercepting any suspicious activity. Mara liaised with allied forces, ensuring their readiness.

At one point, two Commodores arrived, representing allied fleets. Their input was invaluable, providing insights into enemy maneuvers and additional resources for the mission. Kael appreciated their expertise, noting their willingness to stand against Tiberius despite the risks.

By late evening, the final strategy was in place. General Thorne addressed the gathered leaders, his voice steady but urgent.

"We've made progress, but this is only the beginning. Our next step is to secure Lumina. Captain Ventara, your team will lead the vanguard."

Kael nodded. "We're ready, General."

* * *

The journey to Lumina was tense. The Star Fire, accompanied by a fleet of allied ships, navigated through the galaxy's shimmering expanse. Each moment felt weighted with anticipation.

Kael, Riz, and Mara prepared meticulously. They reviewed the battle plans, inspected their equipment, and fortified their commitment. Princess Quann joined them, her presence a source of strength.

"No matter what lies ahead," she said, her voice steady, "we must stand united. For Lumina, and for the galaxy."

Kael nodded, the old motto rising unbidden. "All for one, and one for all."

* * *

The fleet arrived in the Lumina sector, greeted by the sight of its lush landscapes and thriving cities. But the peace was deceptive. They knew that Tiberius's forces could strike at any moment.

General Thorne's voice came through the comm. "Deploy to your positions. Be ready for anything."

The Galactic Trio, alongside Princess Quann, took their positions. The defences were bolstered, and the people of Lumina were prepared for the fight of their lives.

As the sun set, casting a golden hue over the landscape, Kael stood at the forefront, his eyes scanning the horizon. He knew that the battle ahead would be fierce, but with his friends and allies by his side, he was ready to face whatever came their way.

"For Lumina," he whispered, "and for the galaxy."

The first signs of the enemy emerged at dawn. A dark cloud of ships appeared on the horizon, moving with ominous precision. The time had come to defend their home, their people, and their future.

Kael gripped the railing of the observation deck, his heart steady. Beside him, Riz checked his weaponry, while Mara coordinated with ground forces. Quann's voice rang through the comm, rallying the defenders with a speech that left no doubt about their resolve.

"Today, we stand not just for Lumina, but for the freedom of the galaxy," she began, her voice resonating with unwavering determination. "This moment is larger than any one world or people; it is a proof to our shared resolve and collective strength. We do not fight out of vengeance or hatred, but from a place of love— love for our homes, our families, and the ideals that unite us. Across the stars, we are bound by a common destiny, and that destiny is freedom.

"We fight for our future, where generations yet to come can look to the stars and see hope instead of tyranny. We fight for the enduring light of justice that no shadow of oppression can extinguish. We fight for each other, knowing that our strength lies in our unity. The galaxy will not bow to fear; it will rise, brighter and stronger.

"Together, we are unstoppable, not because we possess the mightiest ships or the sharpest blades, but because we hold within us the most potent force of all—hope. Let this day be remembered not as a day of war, but as the day we claimed our future. For Lumina. For the galaxy. For freedom!"

As the enemy fleet drew closer, Kael issued the command. "All units, prepare for engagement. Remember, we fight for what we hold dear. Let's make every moment count."

The battle for Lumina was about to begin, and the fate of the galaxy hung in the balance. United in their purpose, the defenders stood ready to face the storm, their resolve unshaken. For Lumina, for freedom, and for hope, they would fight.

A house divided against itself

is destined to crumble,

for discord weakens its very foundation.

Only through unity, trust,

and a shared purpose can it endure.

It is important to weed out dissention.

Strength

is found in unshaken unity.

Chapter 8
A Spy Among Us

The planet Lumina sparkled under the twin suns, its lush landscapes a witness to the prosperity that Princess Quann had nurtured. However, the current atmosphere was far from peaceful. The Galactic Federation Forces and the Lumina Sector's limited military were on high alert, aware of the ever-looming threat posed by Emperor Dominus Tiberius.

In the command centre of the capital city, the Galactic Trio and Princess Quann stood around a holographic display table. The image of Lumina and its four moons rotated slowly, highlighting the strategic positions of Federation ships hovering in orbit, each vessel representing a different member of the Galactic Federation. Each well-armed ship was place in strategic location around the Lumina sector, officially doing either scientific research or asteroid survey work – ready to pounce into action at any moment. Their presence was a reassurance, but also a stark reminder of the tensions simmering beneath the surface.

"Every Federation nation has a ship here, each with varying levels of expertise and armament," Kael observed, his piercing green eyes scanning the display. "It's a formidable force, but if Tiberius decides to strike, it'll be chaos."

Princess Quann, her blue eyes reflecting profound purpose, nodded. "Our forces can handle skirmishes, but a full-scale war would be devastating. We must rely on the unity and strength of the Federation."

Riz, his typical after five shadow twitched as he frowned, added, "And we have another problem. There's a suspicion that Tiberius has planted a spy among us."

Mara, ever vigilant, placed a hand on her blaster. "We need to find this traitor before they can do any more damage. Every second counts."

The command centre's doors slid open, and General Thorne entered, his presence commanding immediate attention. "We have intelligence that supports the suspicion of a spy within the Lumina ranks," he began, his voice a low growl. "We've narrowed it down to a few suspects, but we need solid evidence."

Kael turned to the General. "What's our plan, sir?"

"We'll start with surveillance and then move to interrogation," Thorne replied. "I need your team to handle the investigation discreetly. We can't afford to alert the traitor."

* * *

The next few days were a whirlwind of covert operations. Kael, Riz, and Mara split up, each taking on different roles to gather information. Kael mingled with the troops, using his charm to subtly extract intel from casual conversations. Riz monitored the base's communications network, his sharp mind spotting patterns and intercepting any suspicious encrypted messages. Meanwhile, Mara, ever the sharp observer, kept a close eye on key suspects, her instincts honed to detect the slightest irregularity.

One evening, as the twin suns dipped below the horizon, bathing the landscape in golden light, Mara noticed something unusual. Junior Lieutenant Bren, a relatively new officer, with no known disciplinary issues, was behaving oddly. He seemed nervous, his head swiveling constantly as if he feared being followed. His steps were hurried and irregular, and his fingers fidgeted with the data tablet he carried.

Deciding to dig deeper, Mara followed him at a discreet distance. Her patience paid off when she spotted Bren slipping into a service tunnel beneath the building—a restricted area that only authorized personnel could access. Mara activated her comm and whispered, "Kael, Riz, Bren's headed into a service tunnel. Something's off."

She moved closer, pressing herself against the cool metal walls to remain unseen. As she peered into the shadows, she caught sight of Bren handing a data chip to a figure cloaked in darkness. The shadowy individual spoke in hushed tones, and although Mara couldn't make out the words, the urgency of their exchange was unmistakable. Her heart raced. She activated her comm again, this time encrypting the signal for additional security. "I've found Bren meeting someone. Looks covert. We need to act fast."

Mara snapped a covert image of the interaction using her wrist device, capturing the figure's silhouette. After a moment, Bren turned and exited the tunnel, his face pale and tense. The shadowy figure melted into the darkness, vanishing through another exit.

She regrouped with Kael and Riz to report her findings. "Junior Lieutenant Bren isn't just nervous—he's hiding something. I caught him passing a data chip to someone in the service tunnels. They're operating covertly, and whoever he's working with is no ally."

Kael's face hardened. "We need to act carefully. Riz, see if you can retrieve the encryption logs from the tunnels' communication relays. Mara, keep tabs on Bren but don't spook him."

Mara nodded. "We'll have to interrogate him soon. If he knows we're onto him, he could blow the whole operation."

Kael agreed, his voice firm. "Let's move quickly. Quietly. We don't want anyone to even suspect that we suspect."

* * *

Bren sat in the small, dimly lit interrogation room, the dim lighting casting eerie shadows on the walls. The single overhead light swung slightly, its motion creating an unsettling ambiance. Sweat trickled down Bren's forehead, his hands trembling on the metal table before him. Kael, Riz, and Mara stood before him, their expressions a mix of stern resolve and unreadable calm.

"Junior Lieutenant Bren," Kael began, his tone even but carrying an edge of authority. "We've noticed some unusual behavior from you lately. Care to explain?"

Bren's eyes darted around the room, looking for an escape that wasn't there. His voice came out strained. "I-I don't know what you're talking about. How am I supposed to know why I'm here or what you want from me. Just let me go and I will be on my way."

Riz stepped forward, his imposing figure casting a large, intimidating shadow over Bren. "Let's cut to the chase," Riz growled. "We can do this the easy way or the hard way. Start talking."

Bren swallowed hard, the vain in his throat pulsed nervously. "I swear, I haven't done anything wrong," he insisted, but his voice lacked conviction.

Mara leaned in closer, her voice a low, almost comforting whisper. "Lieutenant, we have ways of finding out the truth. If you cooperate, things will go a lot easier for you."

The combination of his whining guilt, their domineering presence and words were too much for Bren. His resolve crumbled like a sandcastle before a rising tide. "Look, what do you want from me?"

Kael leaned in closer. We already know about the invasion plans by Emperor Dominus Tiberius but all we need from you is a confirmation of dates and times. If you give us what we want we will let you go free and clear but if you hold anything back, all we have to do is let Tiberious know that you have been telling us what we need to know and then you are dead meat, strung up by the Emperor himself. What will it be, freedom with us or strung up by Tiberius. Personally I like the idea of you being strung up in the main square so everyone can see what a ruthless tyrant Tiberius is. I will make sure your wife and kids see the news item. "Federation traitor strung up naked by Emperor Dominus Tiberius". I am sure it will sell a lot of papers."

Junior Lieutenant Bren started to shake, "You have to promise that you will let me go and I can leave with my wife and kids and never come back. Alright, alright," he muttered, defeated. "I'll tell you what you need to know."

Kael crossed his arms, his gaze piercing. "We're listening."

Bren took a shaky breath. "I was approached by someone who claimed to be a sympathizer," he began. "They said they wanted information on our defences, our troop movements. They said they would pay off my gambling debt."

Kael's eyes narrowed, his tone growing colder. "And you gave it to them?"

Bren nodded, his head hanging low. "Yes. I was desperate. They promised me protection, a way out if things went wrong."

"Who were they?" Mara pressed, her voice cutting through the tension like a knife.

"I don't know their names," Bren confessed, his voice barely above a whisper. "But they mentioned Emperor Tiberius. They were definitely working for him."

Kael exchanged a glance with Riz and Mara, a silent communication passing between them. Kael leaned in closer, his tone now carrying a hint of menace. "You'd better not be holding anything back, Bren. What else did they ask for? What did you give them?"

Bren breathed in and out with panic, fear evident in his eyes. "I gave them a little bit to start. Little pieces of info that would not matter but they demanded more. I gave them more and more until they finally threatened to kill my wife and kids. I had no way out. They wanted detailed schematics of the base, schedules of troop rotations, access codes. I-I gave them what they asked for just to keep my wife and kids alive. I didn't have a choice you have to believe me. They kept holding it over my head that if I didn't cooperate, my family would suffer."

Riz's face hardened, his voice a low growl. "You put all of us at risk for your own selfish reasons."

Bren shook his head frantically. "You don't understand. They had everything planned out. They knew too much. I thought... I thought I could manage it, that it wouldn't come to this."

Mara's eyes softened slightly, but her voice remained firm. "We understand the pressure, Bren. But you should have come to us. We could have protected you and your family."

Kael straightened, a look of finality on his face. "You'll be placed under arrest, Junior Lieutenant. We'll ensure your family is safe, but you'll have to face the consequences of your actions."

Bren slumped in his chair, tears welling in his eyes. "I'm sorry. I never wanted it to go this far."

Kael nodded to Riz, who placed a firm hand on Bren's shoulder. "We'll take it from here."

As they led Bren out of the room, Kael turned to Mara. "We need to find out how deep this goes. If Bren was approached, others might have been too. We need to root out any other spies before they can do more damage."

Mara nodded, the joy of a solid sense of purpose shining in her eyes. "We'll get to the bottom of this, Kael. For Lumina and the Federation."

The team left the interrogation room, their resolve stronger than ever. They knew the battle was far from over, but with the information they had gathered, they were one step closer to uncovering the full extent of Emperor Tiberius's treachery.

* * *

With Junior Lieutenant Bren's confession, the team regrouped in the command centre to plan their next move. General Thorne listened intently as Kael, Riz, and Mara relayed the information they had just learned.

"We need to find this contact," Thorne said. "If we can catch them, we can trace the network back to Tiberius. Is there any chance we can rely on Junior Lieutenant Bren and squeeze him into being a double agent."

Princess Quann, who had be silent until now, spoke up. "I'll help. My presence might draw them out."

Kael hesitated. "It's dangerous, Princess."

"I know," she replied, her voice steady. "But it's a risk I'm willing to take. For Lumina."

* * *

The next day, Princess Quann moved through the capital city with an air of nonchalance, but her eyes were sharp, missing nothing. Kael, Riz, and Mara were close by, ready to intervene at a moment's notice.

As Quann entered a bustling market square, a figure approached her. It was a woman, her face partially obscured by a hood. She slipped a note into Quann's hand and vanished into the crowd.

Kael, watching from a distance, signaled to Mara. "Follow her."

Mara nodded and melted into the crowd, her eyes locked onto the retreating figure.

* * *

The woman led Mara through a labyrinth of alleyways, finally entering a rundown building. Mara waited a moment before entering, her blaster drawn. Inside, she found the woman speaking to a mysterious figure.

Mara's heart raced as she crept closer, catching snippets of their conversation.

"The plans are set," the woman was saying. "We move tonight."

Mara stepped into the light, her blaster trained on them. "Not if I can help it."

The shadowy figure turned, revealing a familiar face. "Commander Vela?"

Vela, a trusted ally from the Freedom Alliance Fighters, looked shocked. "Mara? What are you doing here?"

"I could ask you the same thing," Mara replied, her eyes narrowing. "Explain yourself."

Vela sighed. "It's not what it looks like. I'm undercover, trying to infiltrate Tiberius's network."

Mara lowered her blaster slightly. "Why didn't you inform us?"

"I couldn't risk it," Vela explained. "The fewer people who knew, the better."

* * *

Back at the command centre, Mara and Vela explained the situation to General Thorne, Kael, Riz and Princess Quann.

"Vela was working undercover to get close to Tiberius's agents," Mara said. "She wasn't a traitor."

General Thorne, who had joined them, nodded approvingly. "Good work, Commander Vela. Your actions might have saved us."

Vela, looking relieved, replied, "I did what I had to. Now we need to use the information I've gathered."

Kael leaned forward. "What do you have for us?"

Vela's eyes hardened with resolve. "Tiberius is planning a major attack on Lumina. We need to prepare for it and turn the tables on him."

* * *

The following hours were a frenzy of activity as the Galactic Trio, Princess Quann, and their allies prepared for the impending assault. Ships were armed, defences were fortified, and troops were mobilized.

As night fell, the command centre was abuzz with anticipation. The holographic display showed the approaching enemy fleet, a dark cloud against the stars.

Kael, standing at the forefront, addressed the gathered forces. "This is it. We fight not just for Lumina, but for the entire Federation. All for one, and one for all."

The response was a resounding cheer, unity and purpose were palpable.

* * *

The battle that ensued was fierce and unrelenting. The skies over Lumina were lit with the fire of blaster cannons and the glow of energy shields. The Galactic Trio fought with unmatched skill and bravery, leading the charge against Tiberius's forces.

Riz, piloting the Star Fire with precision, called out, "We've got incoming fighters arriving on your port side. Be ready. They are coming in fast!"

Mara, at the tactical station, responded, "Engaging countermeasures. Hang on!"

Kael, coordinating the defence, issued orders. "Hold the line! Protect the capital at all costs!"

Princess Quann, in her command post, rallied her troops. "For Lumina! For the Federation!"

* * *

As the battle raged on, it became clear that Tiberius had underestimated the strength and unity of Lumina and its allies. One by one, the enemy ships fell, their attacks thwarted by the combined might of the Federation.

In the end, the skies were clear, the threat vanquished. The people of Lumina celebrated their victory, their spirits lifted by the sight of the Galactic Trio and Princess Quann standing triumphant.

Kael, bruised but smiling, turned to his friends. "We did it."

Riz, the stubble on his face, scorched in places, grinned. "Another day, another victory."

Mara, ever stoic, allowed herself a rare smile. "All for one, and one for all."

Princess Quann, her eyes shining with gratitude, addressed the crowd. "This victory is a tribute to our unity, a demonstration of our unbreakable bond with the Galactic Federation. Our friendship, our bond, our pledge to brotherhood is our strength. Together, we will face any challenge and overcome any foe."

The cheers that followed echoed through the night, a celebration of freedom, justice, and the unbreakable bond of the Galactic Federation.

A brood of Garmillian Rats

draws its strength from the brood

just as each Garmillian Rat thrives

within the brood.

Alone, a single rat may struggle,

but together, they are an unstoppable

thriving force bound by reliability,

guided and strengthened by unity.

Chapter 9
Infiltrating Enemy Lines

The Star Fire hummed with quiet anticipation as it glided through the void of space. The crew—Kael Ventara, Riz Talon, and Mara Steeler—were gathered in the conference room, a small circular space illuminated by the dim blue glow of holographic projectors. Princess Quann stood at the head of the table, her expression grave.

"This mission is unlike any we've undertaken before," Quann began, her blue eyes sweeping over the group. "The intelligence suggests that Tiberius's stronghold on Exolara holds not only his latest military plans but also the key to destabilizing the Federation. If we're discovered, it won't just be our lives at stake."

Kael leaned back, arms crossed over his chest. "We've faced worse odds before, Princess. We'll get what we need and get out."

Riz, always the realist, stroked his thick beard thoughtfully. "Disguised as mercenaries will get us through the front doors, but we're walking a razor-thin line. One slip, and it's game over."

Mara smirked, her fingers absently spinning a small blade on the table. "Close calls are our specialty. Besides, I've got a good feeling about this one."

Kael raised an eyebrow. "You had a good feeling about Napol, and we ended up dodging plasma bolts for three hours. Isn't that how you ended up with a titanium elbow."

"Yah, but we survived and my titanium elbow is better than the original one I was born with," Mara shouted back. "If you don't want a titanium plate in your head maybe we should focus on the plan."

The holographic map of the stronghold flickered to life. The fortress on Exolara was a sprawling complex of steel and stone, surrounded by treacherous terrain and patrolled by automated drones.

"Riz," Kael said, "how's the Star Fire holding up? Any chance she can stay hidden long enough to extract us?"

"If we find the right approach vector and keep her running silent, she'll blend into the asteroid field nearby," Riz replied. "But it'll be tight. We'll need to move fast."

Quann stepped forward, her voice cutting through the tension. "Then it's settled. We'll infiltrate as mercenaries, gather the intel, and rendezvous at the extraction point. Let's make sure we're ready for anything."

As the Star Fire approached Exolara, the crew donned their disguises. Kael adjusted the heavy chest armour of a hired gun, its worn plating lending authenticity to their roles. Mara clipped a blade to her belt, her outfit sleek and utilitarian, while Riz's bulk was adorned with a patchwork of stolen insignias.

"You look like you've seen better days," Mara teased, glancing at Riz.

"And you look like trouble," Riz shot back. "Fitting, isn't it?"

Kael chuckled. "Keep it together, you two. We're about to dock."

The fortress loomed ahead, its jagged towers piercing the dark sky of Exolara. Automated turrets swiveled, tracking their approach as Riz expertly piloted the ship into a designated bay.

"Remember," Kael said as the ship settled. "We're mercenaries looking for work. Don't overplay it, but don't hold back if someone gets suspicious."

The ramp descended with a hiss, and the group stepped into the bustling hangar. Soldiers and workers moved with purpose, their movements a demonstration of their disciplined efficiency. Kael's sharp eyes scanned the area, noting exits and potential threats.

A gruff officer approached, his cybernetic arm whirring as he extended a datapad. "Name and purpose?"

Kael stepped forward, his voice roughened to match his disguise. "The Dusk Blades. We heard this was the place to find work."

The officer's gaze lingered on them before nodding. "You're late. Captain Draven's expecting you. Follow me."

Inside the stronghold, the group was led through dimly lit corridors, the walls adorned with propaganda extolling Tiberius's dominion. Mara's sharp gaze didn't miss the cameras tracking their every move.

"This place gives me the creeps," she muttered under her breath.

"Stay sharp," Kael replied. "We're in the belly of the beast now."

They were brought to a briefing room where Captain Draven waited. A towering figure with a scar running down his face, Draven exuded a portrait of menace.

"You're late," he growled. "I don't tolerate delays."

"We had trouble with the Federation's patrols," Kael lied smoothly. "But we're here now. What's the job?"

Draven's piercing eyes studied them before gesturing to a console. "You'll find out soon enough. Report to the barracks. You're on standby until I say otherwise."

As they left the room, Kael whispered, "That buys us some time. Let's split up and gather intel. Meet back here in two hours."

The group dispersed, each taking a different route through the stronghold. Mara found herself in the mess hall, her sharp ears catching snippets of conversation about troop movements and supply shortages. Riz accessed a terminal in a maintenance corridor, using his technical expertise to bypass security protocols and download data.

Kael wandered into a hangar where he overheard two officers discussing Tiberius's plans. "The Emperor's moving on Lumina," one said. "If we secure Auralis, it'll cripple the Federation."

Kael's jaw tightened. He had suspected Tiberius's intentions, but now he had confirmation. Slipping away, he made his way back to the rendezvous point.

The team regrouped in a secluded maintenance room, their expressions tense but determined.

"Tiberius is targeting Lumina," Kael said, relaying what he'd learned.

"I intercepted data on troop deployments," Riz added. "He's mobilizing a massive fleet."

Mara nodded. "And morale here is shaky. If we hit the right targets, we could sow chaos."

Quann's face was grim. "Then we need to act fast. What's our extraction plan?"

Kael grinned. "Riz, think you can trigger a diversion?"

Riz's grin matched his captain's. "Oh, I've got just the thing."

As the team moved to execute their plan, the tension was palpable. Riz planted explosives in key locations, ensuring their escape would be chaotic enough to cover their tracks. Meanwhile, Kael and Mara secured the downloaded data and prepared for their exit.

Quann lingered near a window, her gaze fixed on the distant horizon. "This reminds me of a mission I undertook years ago," Mara said quietly, stepping beside her. "We were stranded on an ice-covered asteroid, pursued by bounty hunters."

Kael glanced over. "The blue-footed barlick story?"

Mara chuckled. "That's the one. We thought we were doomed until I remembered those curious creatures. They're harmless but can't resist a whistle."

"So you whistled," Quann said, intrigued.

Mara nodded. "And they came. Big, hairy creatures with blue feet. They'd been scooping fish from the salt ponds nearby. Their appearance startled the hunters just enough for us to make our escape. Sometimes, survival is about knowing the little details."

Kael smiled. "Let's hope we won't need any barlicks this time."

The first explosion rocked the stronghold, sending alarms blaring. Soldiers scrambled as the team made their way to the hangar. Their path was fraught with close calls. Mara narrowly avoided a patrol, Riz disabled a drone with seconds to spare, and Kael engaged in a brief but intense skirmish with a guard.

Finally, they reached the Star Fire. Riz fired up the engines while Kael and Mara covered their retreat. The hangar doors began to close, but Riz pushed the ship to its limits, slipping through just in time.

As the stronghold receded behind them, Quann exhaled in relief. "We did it."

Kael nodded, his expression weary but resolute. "Now we take this intel back to the Federation. Tiberius won't know what hit him."

The Star Fire vanished into the starry expanse, its crew united in their purpose. The mission had tested their resolve, but they emerged stronger, ready for the battles to come.

Sometimes risk for unity is necessary.

Unity can always bear the weight of dissent

and turn struggle into triumph.

Strength is forged in togetherness,

where each ally stands as a pillar,

ensuring victory through shared courage,

trust, and unwavering determination.

Chapter 10

The Heart of Lumina

The Star Fire wove through the distant reaches of the Lumina Sector, taking a serpentine route to avoid being detected by the Tiberius patrols. Kael Ventara, seated in the captain's chair, studied the star map displayed on the console.

"This is the longest route I've ever charted," Riz grumbled, fingers gliding over the navigation controls looking for the safest rout. His brow furrowed as he added yet another detour to their course. "Tiberius's patrols are everywhere. They're making sure nothing gets through—supplies, reinforcements, even information. It's a blockade without a formal declaration."

"That's his style," Mara replied, checking her blasters. "Squeeze Lumina's lifelines until the Federation can't help. We've seen it before."

Princess Quann, standing at the viewport, watched the stars blur as the ship moved at sub-light speed. "It's more than just lifelines. He's trying to demoralize us. A slow, creeping suffocation." She turned to Kael, her voice firm. "But Lumina has endured worse. We'll resist him."

Kael nodded. "Let's make sure we get there first. Riz, any sign of activity on the scanners?"

Riz shook his head. "Nothing yet, but these cloaked outposts are tough to spot. We'll have to stay sharp."

* * *

The long journey gave way to tense hours. Conversations turned to strategies and memories of past missions. As they approached the capital, Quann's demeanor grew somber.

"It's been years since I've walked the halls of the Lumina Council," she admitted, her tone distant. "I wonder if they still see me as their princess, or if time has turned me into a stranger."

Mara placed a hand on her shoulder. "They'll see you for the sovereign leader you are. Not just a leader, but someone who's fought for them every step of the way. That's what matters."

Kael added with a grin, "And if they don't, we'll remind them why you're the best chance they've got."

* * *

The capital of Lumina was a stunning city of spires and gardens, shimmering under a sunlit dome that protected it from the sector's harsher elements. The *Star Fire* landed amidst a small, private welcoming party—a stark contrast to the grandeur Quann remembered. Still, the sight of her brought cheers from those gathered.

"Princess Quann! You've returned!" a young council aide exclaimed, rushing to greet her. The aide's enthusiasm was contagious, drawing smiles from the crew and bystanders alike. But beneath the surface, the weight of political tension was palpable.

Inside the council chambers, the warmth of the welcome faded. The circular hall was filled with murmuring voices, skeptical eyes casting glances at Quann as she took her place at the centre.

"Princess Quann," one elder councilor began, his tone neutral. "It is an honour to have you back.

However, we must address the pressing question: what makes you think you can lead us through this crisis? You're still so young."

Mara, standing at the back of the room, muttered under her breath, "Here we go."

Quann stood tall, her voice steady. "Councilors, I understand your concerns. I may be young, but I have seen firsthand the price of inaction. Tiberius seeks to destroy not just our sector, but the hope we represent to the Federation. I've faced his forces before, and I know his strategies. I'm here to unite us, to rally Lumina in defence of its future."

"Words," another councilor scoffed, his expression one of skepticism. "We've heard promises before. What can you offer beyond speeches and ideals?"

Kael stepped forward, his voice carrying authority. "She offers action. The Princess isn't here to make empty promises. She's here with a plan, one that's already in motion. We've gathered intelligence on Tiberius's movements, and we have the means to counter him. But it starts with this council standing behind her."

The room quieted. The weight of Kael's words hung in the air. Finally, a younger councilor spoke up. "If you have such intelligence, why haven't we been briefed?"

"Because it's sensitive," Mara interjected. "Tiberius has spies everywhere. We can't afford to let this information fall into the wrong hands."

* * *

As the debate continued, Riz leaned against a pillar at the room's edge, observing. He whispered to Kael, "It's not just skepticism. It's fear. They're too scared to commit."

"We'll change that," Kael replied quietly. "They just need a reminder of what's at stake."

* * *

The discussion turned to Emperor Dominus Tiberius. The holographic display showed his latest stronghold, and as his image appeared, the room collectively tensed.

"So that's the great Tiberius?" Riz said, smirking. "Short, fat, and about as intimidating as a spaghetti meatball."

Mara chuckled. "He's not exactly the picture of galactic dominance. But looks can be deceiving. His mind is what makes him dangerous."

Quann's voice carried a warning. "He thrives on underestimation. That's how he's maintained his grip on power. Don't let his appearance fool you."

Kael studied the projection, his jaw set. "Deceptive or not, he's beatable. And we're going to prove it."

* * *

By the day's end, the council reluctantly agreed to consider Quann's proposals. Though the path ahead was fraught with uncertainty, there was a spark of hope in the room.

Later, in private chambers, Quann sat with Kael, Mara, and Riz.

"That was harder than I expected," she admitted, letting out a weary sigh. "But we made progress."

Kael offered a reassuring smile. "They'll come around. They just need to see results."
Riz raised a glass. "To Lumina. And to proving them all wrong."

The team clinked glasses, a moment of camaraderie before the challenges to come. For Lumina, for the galaxy, they would fight with everything they had. "All for one, and one for all." They all shouted in unison.

True unity is not spoken but forged in trial.

In the crucible of adversity,

loyalty is tested, trust is strengthened,

and only those who stand unwavering

through hardship emerge

as brothers and sisters,

bound by an unbreakable bond.

Chapter 11

The Zetarian Alliance

The hum of the Star Fire's engines filled the cockpit with a soothing rhythm as Riz Talon adjusted the navigation controls. His sharp eyes scanned the glowing holographic map, tracing the edge of the Zetarian Empire's territory—uncharted space for most Federation ships but familiar ground for the Galactic Trio. Outside, the vast expanse of the galaxy stretched endlessly, each star a silent witness to their daring missions.

Kael Ventara leaned over Riz's shoulder, his jaw tight. "Do we have confirmation on the meeting's location?"

Mara Steeler, perched at the tactical station, tapped her console. "Intel puts Tiberius and President Loanus meeting aboard the *Obsidian Sky,* a Zetarian dreadnought. It'll be orbiting Jexus-4, deep in Zetarian space."

Kael frowned. "A Zetarian dreadnought. That's more firepower than we've faced in years. Tiberius is pulling out all the stops."

Riz smirked. "Good thing we're not here to fight them head-on. Subtlety is our game this time."
"Right," Mara quipped. "Because we're so good at subtle."

Kael's lips twitched into a faint grin. "Let's just hope Tiberius and Loanus don't suspect we're onto them. If they do, this mission's over before it begins."

* * *

The Obsidian Sky was a monstrous vessel, its sleek black hull reflecting the distant light of Jexus-4. The Galactic Trio's plan was as audacious as it was dangerous: infiltrate the dreadnought, disrupt the meeting, and gather evidence of Tiberius's alliance with the Zetarians.

Under the guise of being a trade vessel, The Star Fire, was a fragile dot compared to the behemoth hull it approached. Mara's deft hands manipulated the ship's transponder codes, broadcasting a false Zetarian registration.

"We're being hailed," Riz announced.

Kael nodded. "Patch it through."

The screen flickered to life, revealing a stern Zetarian officer. His golden skin shimmered faintly under the dim light of his command deck. "Identify yourself."

Kael adopted a gruff tone. "This is Captain Ralix of the Silver Fang, carrying trade goods for inspection."

The officer's eyes narrowed. "Your credentials are incomplete."

"We've had… technical difficulties," Kael replied smoothly. "If you'd rather explain to President Loanus why his shipment is delayed, I'll gladly turn back."

The Zetarian's expression didn't waver, but he relented. "Proceed to Docking Bay 7. Any deviation will result in immediate termination."

The transmission ended, and Riz exhaled. "Friendly bunch."

Mara grinned. "Let's hope their hospitality improves."

* * *

Inside the Obsidian Sky, the atmosphere was oppressive. Zetarian soldiers patrolled the corridors, their gleaming armour and imposing stature a constant reminder of danger. The Galactic Trio moved in unison, their disguises, stolen from incapacitated guards, granting them access but not safety.

Mara whispered, "Security's tighter than we expected. They must know how important this meeting is."

Kael nodded. "Stay sharp. Riz, where's the meeting room?"

Riz consulted a stolen datapad. "Deck 12, central chamber. Loanus and Tiberius are already there."

They navigated the labyrinthine of corridors, avoiding unnecessary interactions. As they neared the central chamber, the sound of voices reached their ears.

"That's Tiberius," Mara muttered, her jaw tightening. "I'd recognise that pompous tone anywhere."

Kael motioned for silence. They pressed against the wall near the chamber's entrance, listening intently.

* * *

Inside, Emperor Dominus Tiberius's voice rang out, oozing confidence. "President Loanus, this alliance is in both our interests. Together, we can reshape the galaxy, a new order where power reigns supreme."

Loanus's reply was more cautious. "The Zetarian Empire values strength, but our people will not follow blindly. What assurance can you provide?"

Tiberius chuckled. "Assurance? Look around you. The Federation is fractured, its leaders weak. With my fleet and your resources, we'll crush any resistance."

Loanus hesitated. "And if the Federation retaliates?"

Tiberius's tone darkened as he leaned forward pressing towards Loanus. "They won't have the chance. By the time they realise what's happening, it will be too late."

Kael's fist clenched. "That's all we need. I have the recording of their little secret meeting." With a wry smirk he tapped the com badge on his chest, "It has already been transmitted to Federation Headquarters. They will have it within twenty minutes. Do you want to leave or should we disrupt their little party."

Mara smirked. "Subtlety's overrated anyway."

Riz planted a small charge on the chamber's security panel. "Ready when you are."
Kael drew his energy blade, its hum low but menacing. "On my mark."

* * *

The door exploded inward, sending shards of metal scattering across the room. Tiberius and Loanus spun around, their expressions of shock and fury.

"What is the meaning of this?" Tiberius roared.

Kael stepped forward, his blade held high. "The meaning, Tiberius, is the end of your schemes."
Loanus reached for a concealed blaster, but Mara's shot disarmed him before he could aim.
"Don't even think about it," she warned.

The room erupted into chaos. Zetarian guards poured in, their weapons blazing. Riz took cover behind a console, returning fire with deadly precision. Mara activated her plasma shield, deflecting incoming shots as she advanced on Loanus.

Kael engaged Tiberius directly, their weapons clashing in a dazzling display of sparks. "Your reign ends here," Kael growled.

Tiberius sneered. "You're a fool if you think this changes anything."

Kael's strikes were relentless, forcing Tiberius to retreat. Meanwhile, Riz's quick thinking disabled the chamber's security turrets, evening the odds.

Mara cornered Loanus, her blaster trained on him. "Call off your guards, or this alliance ends with your capture."

Loanus hesitated, then signaled for the guards to stand down. The room fell silent, save for the hum of Kael's blade.

Tiberius glared at Kael, his chest heaving. "You think you've won? This is only the beginning."

Kael deactivated his blade but kept it ready. "We'll see about that."

Mara secured Loanus with binders, her gaze icy. "The Federation will want a word with you."
As the Galactic Trio regrouped, alarms blared throughout the dreadnought. Riz cursed. "Reinforcements. We need to move, now."

Kael nodded. "Back to the Star Fire. We've got what we came for. Let's go! Now! Leave Loanus behind. He will slow us down and get us all killed."

* * *

The escape was chaos incarnate. Zetarian soldiers poured into the corridors, their shouts drowned out by the crack of energy blasts and the sizzle of Mara's shield deflecting incoming fire. Kael led the charge with fearless intensity, his energy blade cutting through opposition, while Riz's sharp shooting picked off enemies with unerring precision.

"This is madness!" Mara shouted over the din, her shield generator sparking with the strain of deflecting a volley of blasts.

"It's only madness if we don't make it out alive!" Kael retorted, lunging forward to clear the next corner.

Finally, they burst into the docking bay, only to find the Star Fire surrounded by a platoon of soldiers and automated turrets. Kael skidded to a halt, his chest heaving. "We need a plan, fast," he barked, glancing at Riz. "How quickly can we clear a path and get out of here?"

Riz smirked, a mischievous glint in his eye. "Fast enough. Trust me. Cover me."

Before anyone could respond, Riz yanked a smoke grenade from his belt, pulled the pin, and tossed it into the middle of the docking bay. The room erupted in thick grey fog, shrouding their movements. "Showtime!" he yelled, darting into the haze like a Pentolian Elk outrunning three hungry Targolian Tigers.

"Riz, wait—!" Mara started, but Kael grabbed her arm. "He's got this. Let's keep them off his back."

The two opened fire, their blasts slicing through the haze, buying Riz precious seconds as he sprinted for the Star Fire's cockpit ramp. Without breaking stride, he tapped his com badge, triggering the ship's engines. The Star Fire roared awake, its rear entry ramp lowering just as Riz dove aboard in one fluid motion.

"Riz, status?" Kael's voice crackled over the comm.

"Give me three seconds!" Riz barked as he slammed into the pilot's chair. His hands flew across the console, activating the laser cannons with a precision blast that obliterated the turrets and scattered the surrounding soldiers. "Path cleared! Move it, now!"

Kael and Mara didn't hesitate. They sprinted across the open bay under cover fire, their boots pounding against the metal floor. The dreadnought's heavy artillery locked onto the Star Fire, its cannons charging with a menacing hum.

Kael shoved Mara onto the ramp and turned, firing one last shot at their pursuers before diving aboard himself. "We're in!" he shouted, slamming his fist on the comm panel. "Punch it, Riz!"

"Hold on!" Riz shouted back, his grin wide as he yanked the controls. The Star Fire surged forward, blasting out of the docking bay and into open space just as the dreadnought's artillery fired. The explosion rocked the ship, but it held steady, the stars streaking past as Riz threw it into hyperspace.

Inside the cockpit, the Trio leaned back in their seats, adrenaline still coursing through their veins. Kael exhaled heavily, a grin tugging at his lips. "Riz, remind me to never doubt you again."

Mara chuckled, her shield still sparking faintly on her wrist. "You owe us about a hundred years' worth of apologies, though."

Riz laughed, his voice breathless but triumphant. "I'll buy you both a drink when this is over. Deal?"

The three exchanged weary but victorious smiles, their bond forged even stronger by the fire of their escape.

* * *

But the victory was not without cost. As Riz guided the Star Fire into safer territory, Mara's sharp eyes noticed the blood staining Riz's uniform.

"Riz, you're hit!" she exclaimed, rushing to his side.

"It's nothing," Riz muttered, but his pale face betrayed him. He staggered, his hand clutching his side.

Kael was at his side in an instant. "What the heck were you doing back there, darting into open space like that without giving us any warning? You could have been killed instead of just being turned into Swiss Cheese."

Riz managed a weak grin. "Sometimes a guy has to do what a guy's gotta do."

Kael shook his head, hooking an arm around Riz to help him to the Med-bay. "You're lucky you're still alive."

In the Med-bay, Mara ripped off Riz's scorched shirt, revealing the smoldering wound. She grabbed a package of foaming disinfectant and slapped it onto the injury. The foam hissed as it began to cool and work.

"You idiot," Mara scolded. "We're only the Galactic Trio if there's three of us. There's no point in killing Meatball if it gets you killed."

Riz winced as she pressed the foam deeper into the wound. "Hey! Easy, Mara! Be mad if you want, but don't kill me in the process."

Mara pulled the gauze away, inspecting the wound. "Next time, stay behind cover. We're not losing you to some reckless stunt."

Kael returned to the cockpit, taking the helm as the Star Fire raced away at full speed. Glancing back, he called out with a grin, "Riz, try not to get yourself killed, at least not before we save the galaxy. That's an order."

Riz managed a weak laugh. "Yes, sir."

The trio, though battered, pressed onward, their commitment stronger than ever.

Mara finished bandaging Riz's shoulder. "That is true commitment. Here you are still smiling even while I bandage up a blaster wound that could have killed you, you crazy bone head. We are so lucky that you grew up in a big happy family where everyone got along so well and was so committed to each other. It formed how you are now, a committed bone head."

Riz replied, "Yah I'm committed but it takes work you know, it doesn't just happen in a vacuum. Commitment takes commitment. That might sound funny that commitment takes commitment but it doesn't just happen without work. Love helps but love comes from commitment and commitment fosters love in the end.

Mara patted Riz gently on the cheek. "I guess the pain meds have taken effect. Here you are waxing on like a Tarbolian mother hen talking about love and commitment. You are still a bone head. Close your eyes and get some sleep."

Freedom is never granted freely;

it is earned through sacrifice and vigilance.

Its cost is not borne by one,

but by all who stand together,

willing to worm out shadows of betrayal.

Only in galactic unity

can liberty be preserved

in the face of treachery.

More Shadows of Betrayal

The Star Fire docked at the Federation's orbital station, its battered hull a proof of the harrowing missions completed by the Galactic Trio. Inside, Kael, Riz, and Mara stepped off the ramp, their uniforms tattered but their resolve unshaken. They were met by General Thorne, whose sharp eyes missed nothing, and Ambassador Zane, his composed demeanor hinting at the storm brewing.

"Captain Ventara," Thorne began, his voice as steely as his expression, "you and your team have done commendable work. However, our challenges are far from over."

Kael exchanged a glance with Riz and Mara, his jaw tightening. "What's the situation, General?"

Zane's tone carried a note of urgency. "We have reason to believe that a senior officer, Lieutenant Dane, has been compromised. Recent intelligence suggests he's been feeding crucial Federation data to Emperor Tiberius. If true, this could dismantle everything we've fought for."

"Not again," Riz muttered, shaking his head. "How does this keep happening? What was the Junior Lieutenant's name that we recently caught red handed. Wasn't it Bren? I hope he is still in lockup."

Thorne's gaze darkened. "Tiberius' agents are skilled at exploiting the weak. I have a feeling that Dane and Bren may not be the only agents among us. We need confirmation and actionable intelligence before moving forward."

"And if we find proof?" Mara asked, her voice cold with strength of mind.

"Then we'll act swiftly and decisively," Thorne replied. "Your mission is to catch Dane in the act and uncover the truth. Trust no one outside this room. We have no idea who to trust."

Kael nodded. "Understood. We'll start immediately."

* * *

The next morning, the Trio dispersed across the sprawling Federation headquarters. Riz stationed himself at a secure comm hub, monitoring encrypted transmissions. His fingers flew across the console, intercepting fragments of conversations and scanning for anomalies.

Kael roamed the facility under the guise of conducting routine inspections. His charisma and sharp intuition drew out subtle clues from wary officers. Meanwhile, Mara shadowed Lieutenant Dane, observing his every move with surgical precision.

One afternoon, as the suns' light filtered through the station's reinforced glass, Riz's earpiece crackled. "I've got something," he said. "There's an encrypted message being routed through Dane's terminal. He's using a proxy to mask the destination but I have stopped it. He won't even know that it did not transmit."

Kael's voice came through, steady. "Mara, stay on him. Riz, see if you can trace where those messages we being sent."

* * *

Later that evening, Mara's surveillance paid off. Dane slipped into an unmarked maintenance corridor. Keeping her distance, she followed him into the dimly lit passage. Her heart pounded as she saw him meet with a cloaked figure in the shadows.

From her concealed position, Mara activated her wrist device, recording their exchange. Dane handed over a data chip, his hands shaking. The cloaked figure's voice was low but commanding. "This is your last chance, Dane. Deliver the next data chip or your family will suffer the consequences."

Mara's earpiece buzzed as she whispered, "Kael, Riz, I've got eyes on Dane. He's meeting with someone but I can't see who."

Kael's response was immediate. "Hold your position. We're en route. We don't want the stranger to know that we are on to them. We will pick up Dane after we process the message he sent out.

* * *

Lieutenant Dane's capture was swift and silent. Within hours, he found himself in an isolated interrogation room. General Thorne stood at the back, his arms crossed, while Kael, Riz, and Mara loomed over Dane's trembling figure.

"Lieutenant Dane," Kael began, his voice calm but firm. "We know about the transmissions. We know about the meeting in the tunnels. It's over. Talk."

Dane's shoulders slumped as he stared at the floor. "I don't know what you are talking about," he stammered.

Riz slammed his hands on the table, making Dane jump. "Don't waste our time. The data chip. The encrypted messages. Start explaining."

Sweat beaded on Dane's forehead. "They forced me," he blurted. "Tiberius' agents. They threatened my family. I had no choice."

"You always have a choice," Mara said, her voice ice-cold. "And you chose to betray the Federation."

Kael leaned closer, his tone lethal. "How much did you give them? And who's your handler?"

Dane hesitated, his face pale. "I gave them some schematics and troop movements. They call him Shadow, but that's only the mission name. I don't know who he is. I have never seen him. That's all I know. Please, you have to believe me."

General Thorne stepped forward, his ominous presence stood in front of Lieutenant Dane. "You know much more than you are letting on Lieutenant. We will extract what you know don't you worry. You will spill the rest of the info. Take him to the brig. Isolate him. Keep him far from Bren. We don't want them talking."

* * *

With Dane's confession, the Trio dove deeper into the investigation. Riz decrypted fragments of the intercepted messages, piecing together a trail that led to a larger network of operatives. Mara tracked sightings of the elusive figure known as Shadow, uncovering connections to high-ranking officials.

Kael convened with General Thorne and Ambassador Zane to share their findings. "Shadow isn't just a handler," Kael said. "He's orchestrating a web of spies across the Federation. If we don't stop him now, Tiberius' plans will gain unstoppable momentum."

Thorne's jaw tightened. "Then we'll cut the web at its centre. Find Shadow. End this."

* * * *

The Trio knew the stakes had never been higher. As the stars stretched beyond the station's viewports, they prepared for their next move. Their mission was no longer just about rooting out spies—it was about dismantling the empire of deceit that threatened the galaxy's fragile unity.

Courage is not the absence of fear,

but the willingness to rise above it.

True bravery is borne

in the trust of unity bonded by

'All for one, and one for all.'

In this unity fear is met

with solidarity even against

the most formidable of empires.

Chapter 13
Siege of Lumina

The Lumina Sector stretched out before the *Imperator*, Emperor Tiberius's massive command ship. The emperor stood at the central viewport, his not so impressive stout figure, an unimpressive shadow. The galaxy's most feared tyrant gazed at the bright, sprawling sector, unaware that his plans were about to unravel.

"Begin the assault," he ordered, his voice a low growl. "Show them the might of the empire."

The fleet surged forward like a tidal wave, darkening the stars with their overwhelming numbers.

* * *

On the surface of Lumina's capital city, Princess Quann stood alongside Kael Ventara, Riz Talon, and Mara Steeler in the main command tower. The Galactic Trio's presence was both a symbol of hope and a strategic advantage. Holographic maps flickered with data as officers and soldiers scurried about, preparing for the inevitable onslaught.

"Here they come," Kael said, his voice steady as he pointed to the projection of the incoming fleet.

Princess Quann straightened her shoulders. "This is our home. We'll show Tiberius that Lumina isn't just another sector—it's a fortress of light."
Kael turned to the team. "Mara, coordinate the planetary defences. Riz, take the Star Fire and lead the fighter squadrons. Quann, stay with me. We'll handle ground operations."

"Got it, Captain," Riz said with a salute, wincing slightly as his injured arm brushed against his side. "And don't worry—I'll make sure the Star Fire doesn't lose its shine."

Mara smirked. "If you don't crash it first."

Riz grinned. "Your lack of faith in my piloting is noted."

* * *

The assault began with a roar of plasma and laser fire. Tiberius watched from the bridge of the *Imperator* as his fleet pressed forward. But something was wrong. The Lumina Sector's defences, far from being weak, had been fortified. Blinding bursts of energy erupted from hidden turrets on moons and asteroids, shredding the empire's first wave of fighters.

"What is this?" Tiberius snarled, slamming his fist onto the command console. "How did they know?"

His second-in-command, Admiral Varn, swallowed nervously. "It appears the sector was warned, my lord. Their defences are... formidable."

Tiberius's eyes narrowed. "Then we'll crush them with sheer force. Send in the cruisers."

* * *

High above Lumina, Riz led a squadron of fighters against the imperial fleet. The Star Fire darted through enemy lines, its sleek frame outmaneuvering larger, more cumbersome ships.
"Riz," Mara's voice crackled through the comm, "don't get cocky out there."

"Me? Cocky?" Riz replied, pulling off a barrel roll to avoid enemy fire. "Never."

Kael's voice joined in. "Focus, Riz. The cruisers are moving into position. We need you to disable their shields before they can target the city."

"On it, Captain," Riz said, adjusting the Star Fire's controls. "But if I get a scratch on this ship, Mara's buying me a new one."

"Keep dreaming," Mara retorted.

* * *

Meanwhile, Kael and Quann led ground forces to repel an attempted invasion. Imperial drop ships descended like meteors, unloading waves of soldiers and assault droids. The city's defenders, inspired by their leaders, fought valiantly.

Kael's energy blade hummed as he cut through a line of advancing droids. "Hold the line!" he shouted, his voice ringing with authority.

Quann, armed with a plasma pistol, stood side by side with the troops. "For Lumina!" she cried, her battle cry echoing through the streets.

At one point, a young soldier hesitated, fear flickering in his eyes. Quann placed a reassuring hand on his shoulder. "Courage is not the absence of fear," she told him. "It's standing firm despite it. You've got this."

The soldier nodded, his resolve strengthened, and charged back into the fray.

* * *

As the battle raged, Mara orchestrated the sector's defences from the command centre. She deployed decoy ships to lure the enemy into traps and redirected power to the most vulnerable areas.

"This is Mara Steeler to all units," she said over the comm. "Focus fire on the lead cruiser. Take out its weapons array."

The plan worked flawlessly. A coordinated barrage struck the cruiser, causing it to erupt in a fiery explosion visible from the planet's surface.

In the sky above, Riz cheered. "That's one for the history books!"

"Less celebrating, more flying," Mara said, though a smile tugged at her lips.

* * *

During a brief lull in the fighting, Riz landed the Star Fire for emergency repairs. Kael and Quann joined him, their armour scorched but their spirits unbroken.

"Nice flying, Riz," Kael said. "You almost made me believe you're good at this."

"Almost?" Riz shot back, mock-offended. "Who saved your tail twice out there?"

Quann chuckled. "Twice? I thought it was three times."

Riz grinned. "Thank you, Princess. Finally, someone appreciates my genius."

Mara's voice crackled over the comm. "Stop stroking his ego. It's big enough to block out the sun."

* * *

As the battle reached its climax, the defenders launched a daring counterattack. Using intelligence gathered by the Galactic Trio, they targeted the Emperor's command systems. Explosions rocked the massive ship, forcing Tiberius to retreat.

"We'll meet again, Ventara," Tiberius growled, his image flickering on Kael's comm screen.

"You haven't won."

Kael's response was calm but determined. "As long as we stand together, Tiberius, you'll never prevail."

* * *

With the imperial fleet in retreat, the Lumina Sector erupted in celebration. Citizens poured into the streets, cheering for their defenders.

Kael, Riz, Mara, and Quann stood together on a balcony overlooking the city. The trio raised their hands, acknowledging the crowd's gratitude.

"For Lumina," Kael said, his voice echoing his pride.

"And for the galaxy," Quann added.

"All for one..." Mara began.

"And one for all," Riz and Kael finished in unison.

* * *

The victory at Lumina was a turning point in the war, a testament to the power of unity and courage. But the Galactic Trio knew their fight was far from over. As the stars twinkled above, they resolved to face whatever challenges lay ahead, side by side.

Victory

is not the achievement of an individual

but the triumph of a group

bound by a single purpose of freedom.

When hearts beat as one,

when minds align in unity,

no force can stand against the strength

of a truly united front.

Chapter 14
Another fight for Good over Evil

Riz threw his hands in the air, frustration etched across his face. "You'd think that after all these centuries, mankind would have finally learned from the past. How many times do we need to see it? Good always overcomes evil in the end. But no, some power-hungry megalomaniac like Emperor Dominus Tiberius always gets it in his fat, meatball head that if he amasses enough guns, fleets, or armies, he can accomplish what every other dictatorial thug before him failed to do. It's like history repeats itself because no one's paying attention to the warnings left behind."

Mara leaned back against the control panel, crossing her arms with a cynical smile. "We all learned about Hitler in school, didn't we? The man thought he could remake the world in his twisted image. They didn't teach us about him just to memorize dates and battles. They wanted us to understand the bigger picture, that evil rises again and again, but it always collapses under the weight of its own hubris."

Riz nodded sharply. "Yeah, but after Hitler, what happened? Stalin, Mao, countless others. And here we are centuries later, with Tiberius playing from the same bloody playbook. He thinks brute force will win him the universe. They never learn."

Mara's smile faded into something more somber. "Maybe they never will. There's always someone out there who thinks they're different, smarter, stronger. But history isn't just about battles and tyrants. It's about the people who stood up to them. The resistance. The rebels. The ones who proved, time and time again, that even the darkest regimes can be brought down."

Riz lowered his arms, the tension in his shoulders softening. "So that's it then? We're the next chapter? The rebels standing up to another madman?"

Mara's gaze hardened, her voice steady. "That's exactly what we are. Because if history teaches us anything, it's that good doesn't triumph by chance. It triumphs because someone, someone like us, refuses to back down. So here we are, heading into another battle."

* * *

The Star Fire cruised toward the edge of the Lumina Sector, its sleek hull cutting through the black void of space. Ahead, an armada of Imperial ships loomed—an oppressive wall of metal and firepower blocking the path to freedom. Dominus Tiberius had deployed his fleet to crush the rebellion and seize control of Lumina's rich resources. The Star Fire and its ragtag coalition of allies were all that stood in his way.

"We're outnumbered ten to one," Mara said, her fingers flying over the tactical console. "Their lead ships are armed with heavy ion cannons and reinforced shields. This isn't going to be a skirmish. It's a slaughter waiting to happen."

Kael Ventara, seated in the captain's chair, exhaled slowly. "Not if we're smart about it. Riz, how's our maneuverability?"

Riz grinned, his hands steady on the controls. "The Star Fire's got some surprises left. She's faster than anything they've got. If we can draw their fire, we might be able to open a path for the Lumina defence fleet to strike."

Kael nodded. "Exactly. Mara, I need a full readout on their formation. Find us a weak point."

As Mara analysed the enemy fleet's positioning, Kael addressed the crew through the intercom. "This is it, everyone. We're not just fighting for Lumina. We're fighting for the entire Federation. Tiberius wants to crush hope itself, and we can't let that happen. Stay sharp, stay brave, and trust each other. All for one, and one for all."

The crew responded with a resounding cheer, their resolve unshaken despite the odds.

* * *

The first barrage from the Imperial fleet lit up the void like a supernova. Plasma bolts streaked toward the Star Fire, their deadly glow reflected in the cockpit's glass. Riz's hands moved with lightning speed, executing evasive maneuvers that sent the ship spiraling and weaving through the onslaught.

"Shields holding at seventy percent," Mara reported, her voice steady. "But we can't keep this up forever."

"We won't have to," Kael said. "Riz, take us into the debris field. It'll give us some cover."

The Star Fire dove into a field of shattered asteroids and smoldering ships. The jagged terrain forced the pursuing Imperial fighters to slow their advance, their massive ships struggling to navigate the narrow gaps.

"Brilliant," Mara said, a hint of admiration in her voice. "But they're not giving up."

Kael smiled grimly. "Good. That's exactly what we want. Riz, lead them deeper into the field. Mara, prepare to deploy the mines."

The Star Fire weaved through the debris, leaving a trail of proximity mines in its wake. The first wave of pursuing fighters triggered the mines, the resulting explosions creating chaos and confusion in the Imperial ranks.

"That'll buy us some time," Kael said. "But we need to hit them where it hurts."

"Their flagship," Mara suggested. "It's coordinating the entire fleet. If we take it out, the rest will be disorganised."

Kael nodded. "Then that's our target. Riz, plot a course."

* * *

The Imperial flagship, an imposing behemoth bristling with weapons, loomed ahead. The Star Fire approached at full speed, its engines roaring like a beast unleashed.

"We've got incoming fighters," Mara warned. "They're trying to intercept us."

"Not today," Riz muttered, executing a barrel roll that sent the Star Fire spinning past the enemy ships. Mara's precise targeting took out several fighters, clearing the path to the flagship.

As they closed in, Kael stood from his chair, his voice firm. "Riz, take us under their shields. Mara, focus fire on their engines. Let's cripple them."

The Star Fire dived beneath the flagship, its cannons blazing. Explosions rippled across the massive ship's hull as Mara's targeting paid off. The flagship's engines sputtered, its movements slowing.

"They're launching escape pods," Mara reported. "Looks like their captain is bailing."

Kael smiled grimly. "Good. Send a message to the rest of the fleet: their leader has abandoned ship. Let's see how loyal they really are."

* * *

The tide of battle shifted. The Imperial fleet, disheartened by the loss of their flagship, began to falter. The Lumina defence fleet seized the opportunity, launching a coordinated counter-attack that pushed the Imperials into retreat.

On the Star Fire's bridge, the crew erupted into cheers as the last enemy ship jumped to hyperspace.

Kael sank into his chair, his exhaustion evident. "We did it. We held the line."

Riz grinned, wiping sweat from his brow. "That'll teach Tiberius not to mess with history. He will go down in the annals of good versus evil as a failure."

Mara leaned back in her seat, a rare smile gracing her face. "For now, anyway. But this isn't over. He'll be back."

With an unwavering expression of fortitude Kael nodded, "And so will we. As long as we stand together, we'll keep fighting. All for one, and one for all."

The Star Fire, battered but unbroken, turned toward Lumina, its crew united in purpose and hope. The battle had been won, but the war for freedom was far from over.

History and true strengthis not measured

by how high we climb alone,

but by how many we lift along the way.

When we elevate others,

we raise ourselves,

forging a path where success is shared,

and unity becomes

the foundation of greatness.

Chapter 15

Exposing the Conspiracy

Ambassador Zane's voice echoed through the Council Meeting, "Esteemed members of the Galactic Federation Council, I stand before you today not simply as a representative of Earth or as an advocate for the Lumina sector, but as a voice of reason against the looming shadow that threatens us all, Emperor Dominus Tiberius.

Tiberius is not merely a ruler of his own empire, he is a tyrant that wishes to expand his grip on humanity. He is a power hungry tyrannical dictator in every sense of the word. History has shown us the likes of him before. We need only look to Earth's 20th century, to Adolf Hitler, to understand the destructive path he treads. Hitler, too, rose on a wave of false promises, exploiting the fears and discontent of his people. He manipulated democracy to seize absolute power and then dismantled it piece by piece. Like Tiberius, Hitler's philosophy was one of greed, power, and domination, not unity or shared prosperity.

Hitler understood the power of indoctrination. He corrupted the minds of the German youth, turning children into spies against their own families. He bribed them with promises of rank and privilege, eroding the sacred trust between generations. Similarly, Tiberius uses propaganda and fear to control his citizens, rewarding betrayal and punishing loyalty to anything but his regime.

But let us remember the fundamental truth articulated by Lord Acton: 'Power tends to corrupt, and absolute power corrupts absolutely.' Tiberius, like Hitler before him, is consumed by this corruption. He sees himself as invincible, yet history teaches us otherwise. Evil may rise, but it always falls. It collapses under the weight of its own arrogance and the indomitable spirit of those who refuse to bow.

The great philosopher Mahatma Gandhi once said, 'When I despair, I remember that all through history the way of truth and love has always won.

There have been tyrants and murderers, and for a time, they can seem invincible, but in the end, they always fall.'

Mahatma Gandhi directly states the inevitability of good triumphing over evil. Do you believe this or not? Tiberius seeks to divide us, to pit nation against nation, sector against sector. His tactics are designed to fracture the Federation, to make us doubt one another. But we must not succumb. The strength of the Galactic Federation lies in our unity, in our shared commitment to the axiom that good will always triumph over evil.

Remember the great words of Albert Einstein, 'The world is a dangerous place to live; not because of the people who are evil, but because of the people who don't do anything about it.'

Today, I urge you all to stand resolute. Let us not allow history to repeat itself. Let us honour those who came before us by ensuring that tyranny finds no foothold in our galaxy. Together, we will prove that the philosophy of 'All for one, and one for all' is not just an ideal, it is our weapon against the darkness.

The battle ahead will not be easy. There will be sacrifices. But as long as we remain united, as long as we hold fast to the principles of justice, liberty, and mutual respect, we cannot fail. Let the name Dominus Tiberius be remembered not as a conqueror, but as yet another tyrant who fell before the unyielding force of good.

We will stand together as a single force of good. Our ships are ready. We will prevail. Let me close with these final words by Martin Luther King. "We shall overcome because the arc of the moral universe is long, but it bends toward justice."

Thank you dear brothers and sisters."

The auditorium burst into spontaneous singing "We shall overcome, We shall overcome."

No struggle exists in isolation;

each is a thread in the vast cosmic tapestry.

Every planet,

every country and city,

every individual

contributes to the greater whole,

proving that unity, not solitude,

is the foundation of strength

and survival in the universe.

Chapter 16
The Fall of Tiberius

The galaxy's fate hung in the balance as the allied forces of the Galactic Federation prepared to launch their coordinated attack on Emperor Dominus Tiberius's impenetrable stronghold. Positioned at the heart of the Astaron Nebula, the fortress was a massive, foreboding structure surrounded by a fleet of Tiberius's most loyal warships. It was a final bastion of tyranny, and its fall would signal the end of his reign.

Kael Ventara stood on the bridge of the Star Fire, gazing out at the enemy fleet pondering their fate. Beside him were Riz Talon, Mara Steeler, and Princess Quann, each preparing in their own way for the battle to come. The weight of responsibility pressed on them, but the unity in their resolve was unshakable.

"We've planned for this moment for years," Kael said, his voice steady. "Everything we've fought for comes down to today. Tiberius has underestimated us for the last time."

Riz cracked his knuckles, a grin forming despite the tension. "Good. It's about time we showed that meatball of an emperor what the Galactic Trio can do."

Mara rolled her eyes but smiled faintly. "Focus, Riz. This isn't just another mission. We're facing his strongest defences, his most loyal forces. We can't afford any mistakes."

Princess Quann stepped forward, her voice calm but firm. "And we won't. We have the Federation behind us and the strength of countless worlds that refuse to bow to tyranny. Tiberius's time is over."

Kael nodded, turning to the crew gathered on the bridge. "Prepare for battle. Riz, take us into formation with the fleet. Mara, coordinate with the other ships. Make sure every unit knows their role. Quann, you're with me—let's rally the troops."

* * *

The Star Fire joined the massive armada of Federation ships, each vessel gleaming with readiness as they moved into position. At the centre of the fleet was the flagship Unity, commanded by Admiral Thorne, whose strategic brilliance had united the disparate forces against Tiberius's regime.

Thorne's voice crackled over the comm. "Attention, all units. This is Admiral Thorne. Today, we strike a blow for unity. Our target is the Astaron Fortress, the symbol of Tiberius's oppression. Remember your training. Trust your comrades. Together, we will end this tyranny. All ships, engage!"

The fleet surged forward, their engines lighting up the void as the battle began. Tiberius's forces responded immediately, unleashing a torrent of plasma fire. The nebula's vibrant gases illuminated the clash, creating a breathtaking yet deadly spectacle.

* * *

Onboard the Star Fire, Kael directed his crew with precision. "Riz, bring us around the right flank. Mara, target their turrets. We need to create an opening for the ground assault team."

Riz executed a sharp maneuver, dodging enemy fire as Mara unleashed a volley of blasts that struck true, disabling a key turret on one of Tiberius's cruisers.

"Nice shot," Kael shouted to Mara with encouragement. "Keep it up. We're almost there."
As the Star Fire advanced, the comm buzzed with updates from other ships. Reports of victories and losses poured in, each adding to the intensity of the battle. Through it all, the Federation forces pushed forward, their true grit unyielding.

* * *

Meanwhile, Princess Quann led the ground assault team, her presence inspiring the troops. Clad in battle armour adorned with the sigil of Lumina, she wielded a plasma blade with skill and grace. Beside her were Kael, Riz, and Mara, each fighting with unwavering resolve.

"Stick to the plan!" Quann shouted over the chaos of the battlefield. "We take out their shield generator first. Without it, their defences will crumble."

The team moved with precision, navigating the fortress's labyrinth of corridors. They encountered fierce resistance, but their unity and training saw them through. Kael's energy blade cut through enemy troops with precision, while Riz provided cover fire. Mara's sharp eyes spotted traps and ambushes, ensuring the team's progress remained steady.

At last, they reached the shield generator room. It was a massive chamber filled with humming machinery and guarded by Tiberius's elite soldiers. Quann stepped forward, her voice ringing with authority. "Surrender now, and you will not be harmed. This is your only chance."

The soldiers hesitated, their loyalty wavering in the face of her confidence. But their leader, a hulking figure clad in dark armour, snarled. "The Emperor's will is absolute. You will not pass."

Kael raised his blade, his voice calm but firm. "Then we'll have to make our own way."

The battle that followed was intense, the room vibrated with the clash of weapons and the hum of plasma fire. Quann engaged the armoured leader in a duel, their blades meeting in a shower of sparks. Kael, Riz, and Mara fought the remaining soldiers, their teamwork honed to perfection.

Despite the enemy's strength, the Galactic Trio and Quann prevailed. The shield generator was destroyed in a brilliant explosion, the fortress's defences faltering as a result.

* * *

Back in space, the Federation fleet capitalized on the opportunity. Admiral Thorne's voice came over the comm. "The shields are down. All ships, focus fire on the fortress. Let's end this."

The combined firepower of the fleet unleashed a devastating barrage. The fortress's walls cracked and crumbled, explosions rippling across its surface. Inside, the Galactic Trio and Quann raced against time, navigating the collapsing structure to reach Tiberius's command centre.

* * *

The command centre was a grand, opulent chamber, its walls adorned with symbols of Tiberius's regime. At its centre stood the Emperor himself, a weak figure of a man exuding more arrogance than menace.

"You dare to challenge me?" Tiberius spat, his voice echoing with fury. "I am the master of this galaxy. You are nothing but insects beneath my feet."

Kael stepped forward, his blade raised. "Your reign is over, Tiberius. The galaxy has had enough of your tyranny."

Tiberius sneered. "You think you've won? My empire will outlast all of you. I have built it on power, and power is eternal."

Quann's voice cut through his bravado. "Power built on fear and oppression will always crumble. Your time is up."

With a roar of rage, Tiberius activated his own energy blade and charged. The battle was fierce, the room shaking with the force of their clashes. Kael faced Tiberius head-on, their blades meeting in a deadly dance. Riz and Mara provided support, targeting the Emperor's automated defences, while Quann coordinated their efforts.

Despite his strength, Tiberius was no match for their unity. Kael's blade struck true, disarming the Emperor, quickly forcing him to his knees. Quann stepped forward, her voice steady. "Your empire is finished. Surrender, and you may yet live to face justice."

Tiberius laughed bitterly. "Justice? There is no justice in the galaxy. Only power."

Kael shook his head. "That's where you're wrong. The galaxy is stronger than you think, and it doesn't need you."

As Tiberius was taken into custody, the fortress continued to collapse. The Galactic Trio and Quann made their escape, their mission complete.

* * *

Outside, the Federation fleet cheered as the fortress exploded in a final, brilliant burst of light. The fall of Tiberius marked the beginning of a new era for the galaxy, one built on unity and hope.

Back on the Star Fire, Kael stood with Riz, Mara, and Quann, composed in a posture of relief.

"We did it," Kael said, with enthusiasm. "Tiberius is gone."

"But the work isn't over," Quann added. "We have to rebuild. We have to make sure this never happens again."

Riz grinned. "One battle at a time, Princess. For now, let's just enjoy the victory."

Mara smiled faintly. "All for one, and one for all."

The Star Fire and the Federation fleet set a course for home, their hearts filled with the promise of a brighter future. The galaxy had been saved, but the lessons of the past would guide them as they forged ahead, united in their resolve to protect the freedom they had fought so hard to reclaim.

Unity forms an indestructible bond;

divided, the bond crumbles

under the weight of discord.

When we stand as one,

bound by purpose, trust, and strength,

we do not merely endure

but we rise beyond measure,

achieving greatness beyond imagination.

Chapter 17
The End of an Era

The galaxy awoke to a new dawn, free of the oppressive shadow that had loomed for far too long. Emperor Dominus Tiberius was no more, and with his fall came the crumbling of his repressive regime. Every sector of the Tiberius empire surrendered without resistance, celebrating the end of tyranny. Across countless systems, from the shining towers of Lumina to the rugged plains of Duneara, people celebrated the unity of The Galactic Federation and a shared hope for a brighter future for all. This day of celebration became known as "The Day of Unity".

On the capital planet of the Galactic Federation, an assembly unlike any other was convened.

Delegates from every corner of the galaxy filled the great hall, their voices buzzing with anticipation. At the centre stood Princess Quann, resplendent in a simple yet elegant gown that bore a sash with the insignia of her people. She radiated strength and grace, her mere presence a symbol of resilience.

Admiral Thorne, a towering figure of authority, stepped forward to address the assembly. "Today, we honour the heroes who made this victory possible," he began. His voice carried the weight of history. "The Galactic Trio and Princess Quann stood as beacons of hope in our darkest hour. Their courage and unity remind us of the power of standing together against tyranny. Let us welcome them now. I give you Captain Kael Ventara, Lieutenant Riz Talon, and Lieutenant Mara Steeler. The three of them bashfully stepped forward to thunderous applause, Princess Quann stood at their side. The trio's presence was magnetic, their every step a reminder of their unfailing journey. The applause swelled as they reached the platform, where Admiral Thorne offered them a respectful nod.

Quann spoke first, her voice steady but choked with emotion. "This victory is not ours alone. It belongs to every person who resisted. It belongs to every planet and small outpost that dared to join in unity. This victory belongs to everyone who dared to dream of, "All for one, and one for all". Today, we reclaim not just our galaxy, but the ideals that unite us: justice, courage, and hope. Let us rebuild together."

Her words were met with a roar of agreement, the assembly rising to their feet in a standing ovation.

* * *

While celebrations unfolded, the grim aftermath of Tiberius's fall was being addressed. Imprisoned in a high-security facility, the former emperor awaited trial for his innumerable war crimes. His once-arrogant demeanor was intact, though diminished by isolation. The trial was swift, the evidence overwhelming. Witnesses from countless worlds recounted the atrocities committed under his rule.

But even justice could not quell the twisted mind of Dominus Tiberius. Before his sentencing could be carried out, he ended his life, leaving behind a bitter note devoid of remorse. "The galaxy," he wrote, "was too weak to deserve my vision. You will regret my absence, for I was the only true leader worthy of its greatness."

His death marked the end of an era of oppression. Yet, his final words served as a reminder of the dangers of unchecked power and the resilience required to oppose it.

* * *

Back on Lumina, the Galactic Trio and Princess Quann gathered for a quieter celebration. The Star Fire, their faithful ship, sat in drydock, undergoing repairs and upgrades after the fierce battles it had endured. The four heroes shared a meal in the palace gardens, the atmosphere a mix of joy and bittersweet reflection.

Riz raised his glass. "To victory," he said, his usual humour softened by sincerity. "And to the craziest crew I've ever had the honour of flying with."

"Hear, hear," Mara added, her rare smile lighting up her face.

Kael leaned back in his chair, his expression thoughtful. "We've come a long way. But this isn't just the end of a fight. It's the start of something new. A chance for the galaxy to heal."

Quann nodded. "And you three have given me more than I can ever repay. Your bravery saved my people, and your friendship reminded me that we're stronger together."

The moment lingered, each of them taking in the magnitude of what they had accomplished. Finally, Kael broke the silence.

"I'm sticking around for a few days," he said. "The Star Fire needs some work, and I've got to make sure she's ready for the next adventure. But after that, it's back to Duneara for me. There's still a lot of carmidian ore to be mined. Might be hot and dusty, but it's home." He paused, a faint smile playing on his lips. "You both know the Oasis Bar is always there if you feel like a carmidian cocktail."

Mara chuckled. "I'll keep that in mind, Kael. But don't think this means we're done watching your back."

"You couldn't get rid of us if you tried," Riz added, his grin widening.

Quann stood, her eyes misty as she extended her hands to them. "Wherever you go, know that you will always have a home here on Lumina and in my heart."

A hug of gratitude and unspoken promises filled their lingering embrace.

* * *

As the Galactic Trio prepared to depart, a ceremony was held in the palace square. Thousands gathered to bid farewell to the heroes who had risked everything for their freedom. Kael, Riz, and Mara stood side by side, their bond unshaken by all they had endured.

"All for one," Kael began, his voice carrying over the crowd.

"And one for all," Riz and Mara finished in unison.

The crowd erupted in cheers, their chant echoing the trio's words. As they boarded the Star Fire, Riz turned to shout one last quip.

"I still think we should be called the Intergalactic Trio, you bonehead!"

Kael laughed, shaking his head. "You'll never change, Riz."

The Star Fire lifted off, its engines roaring as it rose into the heavens. Below, Princess Quann watched, her heart filled with sadness and pride. The galaxy was at peace, and the legacy of her friends would endure for generations.

* * *

In the vast expanse of space, the Star Fire soared toward its next horizon. Though the battles were over, the adventures were far from finished. Kael, Riz, and Mara knew that challenges would come again but as long as they stood together, they would face whatever lay ahead.

And so, the Ventara Adventures came to a close, not as an ending, but as a promise: that unity, courage, and friendship would always prevail. The motto that guided them through every trial remained their beacon: All for one, and one for all.

Afterword by the Editor

Still in the blazing wake of adventure, hope and togetherness—even in peril and the possibility of death—we celebrate and cheer alongside the heroes in this Hans Muller new novel, which comes to an end that we all prayed for since the ominous shadow of Emperor Tiberius fell upon the galaxy as a mighty menace to peace, a fear surely readers inevitably felt and wanted to overcome, and a reminiscence of historic facts and events thundering dark and bitter in their minds: a projected image of Hitlerism that Muller ingeniously filters into his story.

In this novel, Muller gives prominence to the need for unity, the need for teamwork so the forces of evil can be confronted and defeated when a solid front stands firm and unshaken despite the colossal threats ahead. In my Afterword to the author´s first novel, I said:

> *Throughout their journey, the Ventara team demonstrated how hope is also a shared force. It thrives in the collective dreams and aspirations of societies.*

Muller efficaciously and intentionally blends hope and collectivism as cornerstones in any endeavor. He ably harmonizes both concepts throughout the saga.

Therefore, the two novels enjoy a cohesiveness of principle evident enough to concretize the monolithic yet rich leitmotif he proposed since the beginning.

Time and again, Muller is teaching a lesson to the new generations, to his readers, a lesson that must be taught no matter what. In the process, the high standards of optimism and cooperation gradually become not only a feature of the characters in the novels but also a feature that he builds into his readership: we adhere to hope too, to teamwork!

The paragraph before the last one in the novel reads:

> *In the vast expanse of space, the Star Fire soared toward its next horizon. Though the battles were over, the adventures were far from finished. Kael, Riz, and Mara knew that challenges would come again but as long as they stood together, they would face whatever lay ahead.*

"*As long as they stood together*" epitomizes the author's leading purpose. May this thesis serve us all, for the future deserves "all-hands-on-deck," confident efforts so the human race survives.

Prof. Miguel Ángel Olivé Iglesias. MSc

Author Bio:

Hans David Müller was born and raised in Berlin, Germany. He was born in, 1960 and moved to a small town in Northern Ontario in 1982. With his unwavering supportive wife Christina, they raised three children; two boys and a girl. They raised two goats, a dog, two cats and a pet pig.

Hans taught his children the values related to, all for one, and one for all and the expectancy of good, and to apply those essential life skills to everything they did. He has always had a strong affinity to his roots and his rich cultural history but with his love for forests, lakes and nature, Canada quickly became his new and beloved home.

He pursued a career in education, becoming a cherished and respected high school teacher, where he taught literature and history for almost four decades. His passion for teaching and storytelling was evident in his dynamic and engaging classes, inspiring countless students to explore their own creativity and curiosity. Upon retiring, Hans finally had the time to indulge in his lifelong dream of writing a novel. Drawing on his extensive knowledge of literature and his fondness for science fiction, in particular the "Star Wars" sagas and the little known sci-fi series entitled "Halo," his imaginative spirit drew him to write his debut novel, *The Ventara Adventures: The Resilience of Hope*. Immediately after the first book was published he started working on this, his second book. His passion for the characters has developed into what he hopes will be an ongoing series: *The Ventara Adventures*.

Photograph by
Christina Müller

A short bio note about the Editor, Professor Miguel Ángel Olivé Iglesias. MSc

– Professor, University of Holguin, Cuba
– VP of the Canada Caribbean Literary Alliance
– Guest Member of the Mexican Association
  of Language and Lit Professors
– Author, Poet, Writer, Editor, Proofreader,
  Lit Reviewer, Translator
– CanLit Scholar

As someone who has spent a lifetime immersed in the stories of daring spacefaring heroes—from the halls of the USS Enterprise to the twin suns of Tatooine—I see in Hans' work the same spirit of adventure that captivated me in my youth. His ability to blend action, emotion, and deep moral questions into a thrilling narrative is a testament to his storytelling talent.

If The Resilience of Hope was about holding onto optimism in the face of adversity, United We Stand is about the power of unity—about the way diverse individuals can come together and accomplish the impossible. This is a story for our times, reminding us that no challenge is insurmountable when we stand side by side.

Hans, once again, you've given us a tale that will linger in our imaginations long after the final page. And to you, dear reader, if you have found yourself cheering, worrying, and celebrating alongside Kael, Riz, and Mara, then know that you are part of the adventure, too.

I, for one, am already looking forward to the next installment.

Sincerely,
Richard Marvin Tiberius Grove
Editor-in-Chief, Wet Ink Books

Title: The Ventara Adventures: The Resilience of Hope
Publisher: www.WetInkBooks.com
ISBN: 978-1-998324-13-2 = 9781998324132
Author: Hans David Müller